OBLIGATIONS TO THE WOUNDED

University of Pittsburgh Press

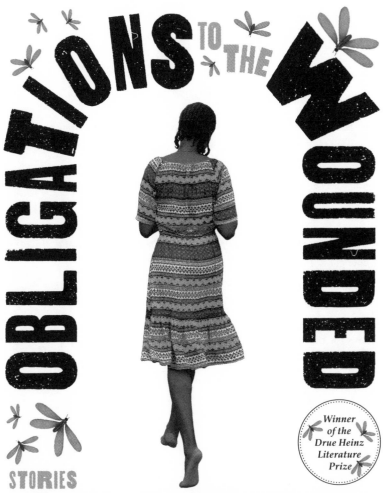

OBLIGATIONS TO THE WOUNDED

TO THE

STORIES

MUBANGA KALIMAMUKWENTO

Winner
of the
Drue Heinz
Literature
Prize

This book is a work of fiction. Names, characters, businesses, organizations, places, events, and incidents are either the product of the author's imagination or are used fictitiously. This work is not meant to, nor should it be interpreted to, portray any specific persons living or dead.

Published by the University of Pittsburgh Press, Pittsburgh, Pa., 15260

Copyright © 2024, Mubanga Kalimamukwento

All rights reserved

Manufactured in the United States of America

Printed on acid-free paper

10 9 8 7 6 5 4 3 2 1

Cataloging-in-Publication data is available at the Library of Congress

ISBN 13: 978-0-8229-4836-0

ISBN 10: 0-8229-4836-2

Cover photo: © Unu Lucky Mamu / Cultura Creative / Adobe Stock

Cover design: Alex Wolfe

For Brad, who believes, no matter what.

And for Moonga and Bilo, who love, no matter what.

CONTENTS

OBLIGATIONS TO THE WOUNDED

AZUBAH

Chakanika bakha nkhuku siingatole.
What a duck has failed to pick up a hen cannot pick up either.
—Chewa proverb

The rhythm of our sisterhood is to call each other frequently enough that we never become strangers.

so far, our system is flawless,

every few months, we swap gossip for a few minutes: *Have you heard Auntie Lu's third husband got their maid pregnant? Perfect cousin Mwape flunked out of law school and is calling himself a pastor! Enhe, yes, 10K Insta followers. His parents are telling everyone how Pastor is higher than Lawyer in the eyes of the Lord anyway.*

When our laughter simmers down, I ask how Azubah is doing, and Chisomo's answer is always "Mama is fine," which paves way for me to race through,

"Okay, I'll send some money for her groceries this weekend."

One of us grows sleepy, a husband or child demands extra attention, and both of us promise-promise-promise, "Sis, I'll call you, mailo," only for the tomorrow to stretch into week after week of memes and thirty-second TikTok videos.

This time, Chisomo bypasses the "Uli bwa? How is the hubby? Na Gabby?" and dives straight into "Funso, Mama is really bad mwe. I think you need to come."

"What do you mean, *she's bad*?" My voice is doing an awful job of veiling the panic racing up my throat,

"Please, sis," Chisomo says, "just come nga you can manage."

Azubah's madness has been brewing for a long time, but not to the extent of the madmen who loiter around Lusaka, lugging around trash like it is expensive luggage and howling family secrets into the night.

On past calls, Chisomo has called Azubah's ailment forgetfulness. Only once has she sprinkled *dementia* into our conversation,

after that, nothing,

so, this murmured *bad*, I take as a rapid unwinding of Azubah's mind, a sudden revelation of her rotten core,

and a siren blares red in my head,

the last time Chisomo said someone was *bad*, she meant Grandpa had died.

In the background, Chisomo's son yells, "I've finished!" and she hangs up.

I'm left staring at the pixelated profile picture of my sister's dimpled smile,

bad: my mind churns the word, assigns it the meaning of Azubah lying depleted, reeking like stale life and Vaseline.
I last took Azubah's call six months ago, last clicked reply to her texts when?

I call my husband, voice not video, because I don't want David's pity-you look to make me cry,

"I mean, I already remit my Black Tax via Western Union with every paycheck." I know I'm whining, but holding it in feels like bile. "What will my presence in Zambia even do?" I say, "If anything, it will make more sense for her to come here, be seen by doctors in a hospital where she can be taken care of properly." Which is to say, in America, I've at least got the option of dropping her off at a sterile assisted-living facility,

David says "I hear you" in that way people do before they show that they are, in fact, not hearing you he says, "but, c'mon, you can't *not* go."

and what I notice is the missing *honey* at the end of his sentence,

"What about Gabby?" my last resort,

surely, my daughter is a good enough reason to stay put,

"Gabby? Oh, she'll be fine. My mom will pick her up from track practice. Mom won't mind."

I'm trying not to shout, trying to do what my Pilates instructor says to do in order to manipulate my mind to be calm, trying to keep my breath steady, sucking in big puffs of air, "Gabby needs her mother, David." It's just a statement, not an accusation, all the air in my lungs makes it so,

"Yeah, but she's your mother, Funso, and *she* needs you," he says,

the first defense of people who actually have mothers, as if the title of mother has no accompanying expectations like care and attention or not abandoning their children for drinking sprees, not moving out when their youngest is nine to live with a faceless father and then a revolving door of boyfriends, only to show up to their daughter's wedding over a decade later with scaly tears and a too-long hug,

"You're right," I hear myself say, my Zambian accent bubbling abruptly to the surface; I clear my throat, "She's my mother."

David likes to be echoed, so, I know that's a smile behind the thawing in his voice, "Then it's settled," he says. "I'll book your ticket. Just tell me when you can get time off, yeah."

I can't speed-walk to the teachers' lounge fast enough, can't grab my thermos fast enough, can't swallow my coffee quick enough, to allow the world to be muffled by the fruit liqueur that I use instead of creamer.

Three weeks of fog float past until I'm sitting in this stuffy cubicle-cum-office-cum-consultation-room listening to a doctor saying,

"Mrs. Ashwood, your mother still has some of her long-term memories. They are just a bit fragmented": in that *I understand* tone salespeople use on infuriated customers demanding refunds they'll never get,
what I hear is that Azubah's whole life is this sped-up movie, with someone else hogging the remote, arbitrarily clicking pause and letting her watch a still shot for a beat before hurtling her into another place and time.

"Pictures will help jog her memory," the doctor continues. "Think of this as you helping her find them. It will probably bring you two closer."

Closer—in a room surrounded by rusting cabinets stacked against the wall. The three of us are seated on creaking chairs arranged in a cramped semicircle, our knees a breath away from touching; a thin illusion of privacy is provided by one babyshit-yellow curtain to my right, but the whole time the doctor's voice is an octave above a whisper, fighting the squeaking tires, rattling medicine bottles, hesitant foot-steps, and distant wailing spilling in from the hallway on the other side of the curtain.

I glance over at Azubah and force myself to smile at her,

she's fixated on a flyer for World Mental Health Day a nurse handed us while we waited for the doctor to come; Azubah is pressing an invisible crease out of the green ribbon embossed to the top of the paper and repeating every second word the doctor says,

the doctor's "You have pictures, right?"

becomes,

"have-right?" in Azubah's mouth,

I have *a* picture; it has lived as a bookmark in a journal I stole from Azubah's purse when I was eleven; journal and book have sat at the bottom of my purse for years,

I cut the doctor a look, "and what *exactly* will she remember?"

the doctor stops fingering her watch and sighs, "as I've explained to your sister already, your mother's condition is severe."

I nod, "and?"

"all of my suggestions will greatly improve quality of life." she nods at Azubah's hands,

Azubah says, "Of-suggestions-greatly-quality-life." and grins like a child proud of something they have done, even though it is stupid,

I say nothing,

the doctor coughs then says, "the Memantine will help her ability to perform daily functions," while updating Azubah's prescription; she hands the small paper to me,

I look at the illegible blue ink and don't ask if she means that Azubah will stop mistaking the sink for the toilet or using the corner of her chitenge as toilet paper and trying to flush down two meters of fabric,

"the Donepezil will help her to interact with others." she clips the pen back into the pocket of her scrubs,

she stands, draws the curtain open, and waves us out, and yells, "Next!" into the crowded hallway.

By the time we slump into the car, I can smell my sweat, the AC spits out dust motes and a warm breeze, but I suck in the air and start Chisomo's car,

I feel about ten again, trying but failing to comb my hair into a puff that will pass the smartness test at the school assembly, frustrated by every curl springing out of my head, wanting to chop off every stray strand out of my control.

Ten-year-old me shakily dials my big sister's number and groans into the phone when she says, "Yes, Funso, hi! How did it go? How is Mama?"

this brittle little laugh escapes my throat, "The good news for her is, she won't remember any of it. Fucking fantastic for her, isn't it? She gets to forget!"

"Funso, naiwe," my sister chides, "think how horrible this whole thing must be for Mama."

"For Mama, ehn?" I chuckle, "When you said she was bad, I thought she was—"

"God forbid! Do not even think about finishing that sentence."

"Then I'll say this, Chisomo. This isn't horrible enough if you ask me. Azubah can't remember a thing. A fucking fresh start for her, isn't it? Must be fucking nice! And what ab—"

"First of all, Funso, that is our mother you're talking about. You can't call her by her first name!"

AZUBAH

"I can call her whatever the fuck I want."

"And for goodness' sake, enough with the swearing. If you insist on using that kind of language, don't do it around Mama. This is not America."

and *there* it is,

where our rhythm ruptures and our affections stutter, this is why Chisomo and I don't send each other pictures of our homes anymore, because where I think I'm showing my sister the miracle of me growing a plant for the first time, she sees my car in the driveway and text back, "New ride? Must be nice," the sarcasm leaching from the screen,

I ease the car onto Great East Road, where traffic is crawling, there's a roadblock staged ahead with two battered drums, I dig into my purse, "take this kwacha for some Coca-Cola, officer," to the policeman, and steer on.

"Damn right, this isn't America!" I spit into the phone,

but where else could I drive without the tension in my fingers, with whiskey in my cup holder, confident that I won't end up in some dingy cell or painted onto a placard at a #Justice4Funso march?

guess there really is no place like home,

Azubah doesn't notice the commotion, she's rolled down her window, is counting the approaching cars like she's reciting the two times tables all mixed up, she waves at a hawker weaving through traffic with a bucket of ripe mangoes balanced on her head, and says "ka mango for a kiss?"

I'm not sure if the hawker hears her, but she smiles and starts jogging toward us,

Azubah pouts her lips and tosses the woman a kiss,

I'm swatting down Azubah's arm, mouthing *sorry* at the hawker, and shaking my head when my sister says, "Yes, yes, we know, Funso. We know this is not your great America." in her mouth, *America* is given the shade of the puddles that have made a home of the tarmac on the road,

"That's what you want to fight about?" I scream, immediately annoyed with myself, we've been apart so long, I've forgotten my way around a fight with my sister,

"Stop it, Funso, naiwe. This—" Chisomo's voice splinters, apparently having trouble remembering our brawls as well. "This is rubbish."

"Agreed. Fu-cking rubbish, you can say *fuck,* big sister. Azubah would never do anything to you."

"Ah, you've started. I thought you came back to help me take care of Mama."

I reach for the open thermos in my cup holder and take a swig,

it's so much easier to be nice to my sister with an eight-hour difference between us, "I *am* helping," I say, "but you're babysitting her at the next appointment."

"You have only been here a week. This was your first hospital visit—"

"Enhe, and?"

"And you know I have to work and they will only see her during the week and my boss won't let me get time off. But you know what? It's okay. I'll take care of her. I always have anyway. Can you just do what the doctor said for now?"

"Fine."

so here I am now, trapped between the same peeling walls of our child-hood bedroom, where I used to hide when Azubah wasn't in the mood to tolerate my face with anything less than a biting backhanded slap. Here, I'd practiced to near perfection how to endear myself to my mother by borrowing the softness in Chisomo's voice, waiting for Azubah to call me out.

Some of my Black Tax pays an old woman to polish the floors and sweep the cobwebs out of the corners once a week so that Azubah can still call this place home,

I'm the one holding the remote control to stop the film at the photo of us from that long-ago place,

Azubah blinks at it, then refocuses on a fly buzzing around the hot room: she smiles at it missing the open window and slamming head-first into the glass and says, "Sorry, baby, sorry," so tender I want to scoop the words from the air and make them mine.

Instead, I hold the picture between us,

in it, Azubah leans against the bark of the cedar that stood guard in the middle of my grandfather's yard, wearing what used to be her favorite puff-sleeved blouse, grinning at me out of a dog-eared snapshot of twenty-five years ago,

the nights I stayed up listening to the choir of owls, crickets, and dancing branches, I'd catch Azubah admiring her reflection in the cracked mirror that hung above the chest of drawers as she painted her face,

blackened, surprised eyebrows,

cheeks the color of my tongue after licking too many cherry-flavored lollipops,

mouth, a blend of her blue eye shadow and crimson lipstick, which created the same exact purple as that puff-sleeved blouse,

the first time I remember her wearing it out in the sun was the morning of my confirmation Mass,

after all the confirmands had marched out and their parents tried to outdo each other with bouquets of wilting roses and gift baskets stuffed with bow-tied teddy bears, a set of beaming parents stopped us at the church steps,

the woman touched Azubah's shoulder and asked, "That lipstick is so pretty, una igula ku?" all the while looking from my empty arms to Azubah's face,

Azubah arched one round brow and said, "This?" pretending to try and remember, "Oh, just one of these tuntembas on the side of the road. Cheap things can be so beautiful sometimes,"

she tossed her head back, flashed the woman her *I use Colgate* smile because Azubah is God's favorite, and he had taken the time to arrange her teeth properly, instead of forgetting and leaving a lisping gap between the top and bottom rows like he'd done with mine,

Azubah's smile crinkled her eyes and put her rainbow eyelids on display, she opened one eye and aimed her wink at the man,

"Oh!" the woman exclaimed, reaching for her husband's arm, nudging their child and rushing toward the crammed car park as if Azubah was this frightening peacock that would devour them,

to their retreating backs, Azubah cackled, like she was watching an episode of *Mr. Bean* on Saturday night TV,

that laugh, which is the texture of munkoyo perfectly brewed and chilled, I still can't re-create it, can never quite get the cadence right,

pride had swelled my chest so much I thought I'd pop,

if you'd asked me on those church steps what I wanted to be when I grew up, I'd have told you I wanted to grow out of my body into a woman who could look as magnificent as my mother did while telling that lie,

Azubah leans in to examine the picture again,

I can smell her now,

she gives me that gorgeous fucking smile,

and my heart grows feral at the sight of it,

I feel robbed,

I came back here expecting Azubah to be like nothing worth wanting,

but no, she still smells like just-out-of-reach cocoa butter hugs,

I grab my drink and take a gulp,

nothing like whiskey to calm gate-crashing feelings,

I nudge her with "Mwaba ziba aba?" pointing first at her puff-sleeved younger self, then at my older sister, Chisomo, and then at me bulging between the two of them,

she squints at the picture, as she's wont to doing when she thinks she's the one being told a lie, like:

No, Mama, I didn't use your nail polish as watercolors.

or

I didn't bury my new school shoes in the garden with the maize to avoid school.

and

Yes, I did bite Chisomo's ear until it oozed red, but only because she said you are not my real mother. She told me that you bought me from Mwaiseni (and I was afraid she might be telling the truth),

Azubah shifts a little and fixes her attention on me,

which instantly mutates the cushion beneath me from velvet to pins and needles, but that picture—us together—is my anchor, keeping my fingers from quivering too much.

She snatches her gaze away and hugs herself. "That is a picture!" she whisper-shouts,

I reach for the voice I used to use on my daughter when she was in kindergarten, gifting me pencil drawings labeled *Best Mom Ever!*

"Yes, this *is* a picture. Do you recognize these people in it?"

she grows visibly small as her gaze clouds over,

"Do you know who is in it?"

Azubah starts to shake her head, stops, beams, and says, "Girl!" then reaches over to caress the spot where a wilted petal had landed on the top of her shoe, seconds before the cameraman clicked,

something flickers in her eyes, and I almost think she remembers me using that flower as an excuse to touch her just after it landed in the folds of her skirt, a touch and "Let me help you, Mama," traded for one more whiff of her because I knew that those nights Azubah whipped up color with lipstick and eye shadow, she first lathered her dewed skin with cocoa butter lotion and then spritzed her wrists and hair with perfume from a bottle shaped like the silhouette of a naked woman,

I've scoured CVS for that fragrance, but the attendants can't help me without a name and I can't describe the smell of a cuddle waiting for me at the edge of a nightmare on the mornings Chisomo and I awoke to her holding us like a treasure that was at risk of being stolen.

There wasn't enough time between the crouching cameraman saying "Ready?" and clicking the moment in place, for Azubah to push me away—

instead, she'd cupped her palms around my head, dug her fingernails into the flesh under my ears, turned me to the camera while she and Chisomo said, "Cheeeese!"

afterward, she slowly released my skin before she turned to navigate the pebbled pathway back into the house,

I let out a shrill howl until my grandfather, smoking on his rocking chair by the bougainvillea shrub that fenced our yard from the next, called me over, handed me a lollipop to stop the tears, and cradled me in his lap.

In the picture, Grandpa is reduced to a grainy point in the corner, just the tip of one of his shoes, if I close my eyes, there I am, sobbing into him while the cigarette smoke stings my nostrils,

Azubah gives the picture another look, this time, she's wearing her worry face, her bottom lip completely sucked into her mouth, gnawing it slowly,

hope flutters in my chest,

she should carry the burden of all these memories, not me,

"Azubah," she says carefully, "Uyu ni Azubah," she insists,

only she's pointing at me and not her,

I take another swig of my whiskey, drawl out the "No." I exhale and say, "*You* are Azubah."

thickness squeezes my throat, calling her Azubah to her face feels like I've been caught stealing a piece of meat from the pot,

she simply shakes her head, *no*, and repeats herself firmly, "*This* is Azubah."

this part is like dealing with Gabby as a toddler, who would double down on everything she thought she knew; wearing two left sneakers, the zipper of her dress in the front, or pouring orange juice, not syrup, over her pancakes, a shaky "Mama?" slips out of me, followed by an even wobblier "why do you hate me?"

the voice is a distant me, kneeling to make eye contact with my daughter, pleading, "Why won't you do what Momma says, Gabby?"

Azubah says, "I hate—" and drifts off,

my heart is raging in my ears,

"I hate you," she says it all quiet, a smirk about her face,

my vision blurs, my mouth falls open, but the words will not form, so I fill it with what's left of my whiskey and consider leaving, but the room starts to carousel,

this is when I understand that you can know a thing and still, it can be untrue.

In a distant memory, I can still hear Azubah calling Chisomo back into the house after lunch,

still smell the hot dough as she gives Chisomo the last chitumbuwa while I continue playing along the road,

I can feel my temples throb where she pulls my hair into a puff, vengeance seeping from her fingers, but to hear hatred stated so starkly,

the three words arranged so neatly, one after the other, is a fresh pain altogether,

for years, I used to confess this suspicion to Chisomo, whispering, "I know she hates me," but only after our bedroom light was switched off and I couldn't see what accompanied my sister's quiet response,

"Don't say that. Why would a mother despise her own child?" Chisomo would say,

foolishly, I still ask, "Why, Mama?" as if the answer will matter,

Azubah turns to face the wall,

an urge to hold her creeps over me, I want to soak in her smell,

I wish I had photos of those times she licked a finger and wiped a crust from my eye or said, "Well done," for passing number one at school, again,

I reach for her shoulder,

she shakes me off and aims to slap me,

I duck,

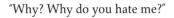

"Why? Why do you hate me?"

"Liar!"

"Mama?"

she presses her hands to her ears and lets out a screech,

now Azubah's vocal cords do the same thing my grandfather's used to on the nights he had nightmares after Azubah left us,

for months, he sleep-walked while shouting her name, calling her a demon before passing out in the hallway,

Chisomo and I would find him splayed there when one of us needed to use the toilet, and we made a game of jumping over him just close enough that we almost landed on his hands,

"Azubah?" she says, nodding at the picture and then at me, the rage of moments ago is supplanted by a wanting look in her eyes,

my shoulders drop,

if I can answer to Marisol and Macey and Marcy at work, I can respond when my mother is calling me, even if it is by the wrong name,

"Ma," I say,

she makes a 360, "Azubah has baby girl," she says. "she loves baby girl," and smiles again,

"Yes," I say, wiping snot from my nose and scrambling for my phone, "That's Gabby," I'm showing Azubah my wallpaper on the screen, which is the only way she's ever seen my daughter,

Azubah pinches her nose, shakes her head, says, "No, Gabby bad," at Gabby circa 2014, holding a Doc McStuffins stuffy in her arm, grinning at the camera, when she was still mommy's baby and loved watching me act out "Little Red."

"No. This is Gabriella. My daughter, remember?"

"No!"

I scroll to a more recent one, Gabby sulking, with her arms folded across her chest, standing next to David at MSP airport. Because it makes me smile, this version of Gabby, upset that her mother is going away, even though she's too grown for me to pick her clothes or plait her hair,

"He will hurt her also," Azubah brings a finger to the screen but avoids touching it, like a hot stove,

"Gabby?" I say, flung back to the memory of me pointing out the name Gabriella to David, from a book of girl names my mother-in-law had gifted me for my bridal shower; he'd already rejected Chimwemwe and

Temwani because who cared that those names meant joy, he didn't want anything too difficult for his family to say,

I set my phone aside, "Who *exactly* will hurt Gabriella?"

She picks up the picture, points to the shoe in the corner, "Gabriel," she says,

"Grandpa? Grandpa will hurt Gabriella?"

she nods,

I know what all the Google articles say, I'm supposed to look past Azubah's nonsense because everything is just a symptom of the disease, not her speaking, but I want to shake her until her brain lodges back into place,

I kiss my teeth, "You're doing this on fucking purpose, Azubah. Why would you say that?"

the memory of my grandfather curdles,

in this playback, it's just me leaping over him in the hallway, Chisomo is snoring softly in our room, Grandpa's eyes are mine, shock-wide with lashes that mostly curl downward instead of up, his nose, hooked and matching mine, makes all the "you look so much like your grandfather, Funso!" knock all the air out of me,

"That girl on your phone," she ventures, "she is your baby, ehn?"

"Yes. Yes!"

Azubah darts her eyes around the room,

"Who put her in you, that small baby?" she whispers. "Was it—was it, Gabriel? Did he make that?" she shuffles, starts to scratch her arms,

the memory sours and my grandfather is facing up at me, I'm stepping lightly now, trying not to disturb him,

"Stop it." It is supposed to be a confident instruction but emerges as a scream,

"He will enter her bedroom at night and plant one in her stomach," she says,

the scream again, "He raised us, you know? While you were gone, he collected our report cards—replaced worn shoes—fed us—everything. And you?"

then the tears come,

liquid words for:

While you were gone, Chisomo had to show me how to fold the cotton wool so I didn't bleed through when I walked home from school on my heavy days.

and

Do you know that Grandpa could never remember to replace the combs when the teeth broke off? Do you know this is why I still cut my hair?

I jab a finger into her chest, "Where were you, Mama?"

but Azubah blinks and vanishes back into herself again,

there is that grab-your-man-off-the-church-steps smile pointed at me, her voice saying, "keep her safe, Azubah, don't let him near your baby," but her eyes are staring out as if into a splice of time only she can see,

here my memory scatters,

there is grandfather, there is Chisomo, there is Azubah, and there is me,

arms are everywhere, bodies pushing and recoiling,

all the articles say that I should empathize, that I should help her through her confusion with kindness and patience, nine-year-old me wants to bury my nose in her hair and tell her, "It will be okay."

"Sorry, baby," Azubah sobs, "sorry."

me? I say, fuck empathy, I lift my purse and walk out into the waiting sunlight,

INSWA

Bwenzi la iwe ndi la wina.
Your friend is another's.
—**Chewa proverb**

When I was thirteen, my best friend, Wongani, kissed me.

In those delicious seconds, while her coal-black lips were pressed on mine, my stomach exploded into an army of golden flying termites, spilling out of their underground castles after a December storm.

My skin burned with tingles all over, and I jerked back from her, unable to place the feeling. *Joy or shame?*

I scanned the sprawling savanna for prying eyes but found only the wide, dusty road wedged between two endless groves of sausage trees.

Wongani clutched her plastic bag of schoolbooks to her chest, leaning back and grinning. "How did that feel?"

But, how to say—my ears were filled with bees fighting to escape? Or that my head felt something like plunging face-first into the Luangwa River? In any case, my mouth had started to shiver and my eyes found home in the impression of her budding breasts through the edges of the transparent bag.

"Well?" she said, shifting her balance from foot to foot.

"Like inswa," I blurted, describing the termites that swarmed Mutengo Village after the rains.

She eyed me for a moment, which only made the flutters in my stomach worse. And just when I thought I'd be torched by her gaze, like an ant cornered by the sun and her mirror, Wongani tossed her head back, the way the older women did when they stopped for each other on their way to and from the fields. The sound of it scattered some birds from the branches of a tree.

No, *joy* did not quite describe it, the swelling in my chest. This was like sucking the juice out of a mango and letting the yellow liquid slither between my fingers. This was a cooling balm against braids woven too tight the night before school. This was sticky beef trotters and beans hot on my tongue against the biting cold of mid-July.

She knelt to pick up a brass coin and used it to draw a square around the edges of our feet, coating our ankles with a fresh layer of dust in the process. "This is our inswa box, Njemile," she said, flipping me the nickel as she spun to face our village.

I ran my fingertips over the head of President Kaunda on the five-shilling coin and read the legend out loud, "Twenty-fourth of October 1965."

She started back for home, arousing delicate clouds of brown in her wake and letting me run after her to catch up like nothing had happened.

Since our first days together, toddling between our mothers' mud huts, that was Wongani's way: to do the unexpected and act like it was ordinary.

"Tiye," she said, hurrying me to her side.

I savored the lingering salty taste of her mouth on mine and nodded.

Holding clammy palms, we skipped back home, using the same route as always: past Headman Amutengo's brick house in the thatched nsaka at the center of the village until we arrived at our matching huts, separated by only a few footsteps. By then, the inswa had spread to my fingertips and the edge of my toes.

Each time we kissed after that day, they fluttered; yet her lips closed off any questions, and I had a few.

Is this allowed? I'd never seen my parents do it.

What if we are discovered? We both knew what happened to girls who made their fathers so ashamed that they beat their wives.

Have you done this before? I hadn't, though catching a glimpse of it at the wedding ceremony of the chief's daughter last year had made me giggle all the way home.

How do you make me feel this way?

Then, as we approached the end of a hellish summer, my mother discovered Wongani and me beneath a wild loquat tree. Wongani and I had stopped for shade on our way back from fetching water at the Luangwa. The buckets were still on our heads, water wetting our faces as they bobbed. By then, Wongani had taught me to open my mouth, to let her tongue slip between my lips and dance wildly between my teeth. I'd learned to suck on hers, swallow the fluid in my mouth and push my tongue against her lips and lick it over and over like a mop wiping a wet floor.

My mother's skin flashed from soaked-earth brown to ash. Her wide eyes became slits. "Mucitanji mweo?!" Either my mother had just asked what we were doing very, very slowly, or time was slowing way down. She was stretching her words and snapping at the same time, like bubble gum.

"Paliye," a chorused mumble from Wongani and me.

"You call this nothing," she rage-whispered, the disgust slipping from her face now into her voice. "A girl, kissing a girl?"

My stupid head refused to stay still. The bucket on my head swayed slightly, water spilling down the sides, a pool of mud forming at my feet.

I should move. My own voice in a faraway place in my head.

My mother, meanwhile, reached into the tree and snipped a thin branch, sending clusters of the ripe brown fruit tumbling onto us.

I knew what was coming next, yet still could not bring myself to move.

"And just where did you learn this…this…thing?" she asked through gritted teeth, waving the whip in the air.

I shot Wongani a look. She bit her lips, staring quietly at her feet.

My mother's question pressed itself in the air around us, stuck to my skin, and became shame slithering down my spine. I wanted Wongani to speak up for me the way she did at school when one of the big girls tried to corner me behind the classrooms for a fight. I wanted her to laugh that big-woman laugh of hers and destabilize my mother's simmering anger. And then, buried deep beneath that, was my laughter, aching to escape. I wanted to be okay with the inswa-flutters on my inside when our lips touched. But my mouth, like my feet, was as still as stone.

My mother gripped me with her free hand, and the bucket toppled, splashing us both. Me, to my waist, her to her knees.

I heard the cracking of sticks that told me Wongani had moved away from the kerfuffle, but, as Amama thrashed my back, the world blurred into the fiery patterns of her chitenge wrapper and the pain jumping across my back and something tight knotting itself in my chest.

The staccato of footsteps that must have been Wongani's dimmed into nothing.

"I! Should! Never! Catch! You! Doing! That! Again!" Each word accented by the whip landing on my back.

"Amama," I whimpered.

"Do not Amama me," she said. "Uninvwa?" She tossed the stick aside.

Every animal in the bush had heard her. Every ant carrying a heavy load across the hot ground, everything all the way up to the wide-open skies.

"Yes, yes," I said between sniffles, wiping away mucus with the back of my arm.

"Good! Because I promise you, Njemile. I did not pray for a child for God to give me one who would dress me in the shame of abomination instead of pride. I"—she pointed at herself—"I mothered a child, not a wild animal. Uninvwa?"

She kissed her teeth, patted her chitenge down, and rearranged her shirt, skipping a button in the middle so that her skin was visible. Her breath was as quick as mine. "In fact, Njemile, I should tell your father, let him deal with this. But as you know, his hand will not spare you like mine. Pick up that bucket and fill it again. Water will not fetch itself, will it?"

Blood rushed to my face. "Yes, Amama."

She stormed off, leaving the threat looming.

For days, her warning hovered over me like a rain cloud, refusing me peace while I did my chores.

At dawn, while I swept the crumbs and arranged cooking utensils in the chigugu, I confused the creaking of the metal door for Atata's leather belt cutting through my skin.

At noon, while weeding Amama's bonongwe, her wild-spinach garden transformed into the sharp strokes of Atata's thin fingers slapping me.

At dusk, the crackling evening fire was the lash of his belt across my back.

But Wongani, in her carefree way, went about as though nothing had changed, taunting me with "Give me inswa" whenever we were alone.

"Why do you do that?" I complained one afternoon as we walked home from the river.

She raised an eyebrow. "Ah, ah, cha?"

"Wongani, if Amama finds us again, she will tell Atata, and you know how he—" The words latched in my throat. I clicked my tongue, redirecting my attention to steadying the shaking pail of water on my head.

Thunder ricocheted through the blackening skies.

"She won't catch us."

"Eh? And how can you be so sure?" My bottom lip quivered, and I started to cry.

Wongani placed her bucket and mine on the ground, then hid both in the bushes. "Listen, I found a place where they won't see us."

I eyed her, unsure.

"Just come."

"Wongani, you can't shit in this village without the flies directing someone to where you are. What place could you have found that no one knows?"

34

She shrugged and said, "Where no one will think to look," then winked.

I followed her into the grass, feeling it grow beside us, the road disappearing behind us.

"You know there could be wild animals in here?"

"In the maize field?" She chuckled. "If there are any, and you keep talking like that, they will hear you and eat us both. Shut up and come." She pulled me toward a huge gray rock that broke the monotony of the meter-high stalks. The stone bent into a cave, barely big enough for us. As we sat inside, my weeping subsided.

Wongani drew a line with her big toe from one end of the cave to the other, turned to me, closed her eyes, purred, "Give me inswa," and I dissolved.

What I wanted to ask: *When did you find this?* I wanted to remind her how Amama watched the sun for how long it should take me to walk to and from the river. There was supper still left to be cooked, and we had social studies homework that day. Instead, I sank my feet into the warm soil, leaned in, and planted my parched lips on hers. Through our T-shirts, our hardened nipples grazed, sending shivers coursing through me, dissolving the rock of fear in my pit. Just then, the skies opened and poured.

Our new inswa box became the final destination of every day.

If Amama wove my woolen braids too tight: "Give me inswa."

If she chided me for spilling too much water on my way from the river: "I need some inswa."

And the growing maize stalks only made it easier for us to hide.

One day, while tilling the fields with our mothers, Wongani and I snuck away to the inswa box.

"Open your mouth," I murmured.

As my tongue found hers, the inswa spread around my belly, threatening to flee through the space between my legs.

I squealed and tumbled out of the secret place, where I met Amama's disgusted face.

"Amake Wongani!" Amama's shout for Wongani's mother was a wild thing, but Wongani didn't seem even half as afraid as I.

Thumping followed as Amama's friend came running.

"What?"

"Take your satanic child away!"

Breathless, she said, "What—satanic—why?"

"She wants to spoil my child. Please if…if this is how you are raising your own, not mine—"

Amake Wongani's voice returned. "Wait," she said, looking from her daughter to me and then back at Wongani, settling there with something akin to exhaustion. She sighed. "What are you saying?"

"Ask her," Amama snapped. "But meanwhile, keep her from mine."

Amake Wongani blinked slowly, then turned to glower at me before half dragging her away.

She will tell him now, I panicked.

"Amama," I begged, "Atata, please." The sentence was disarranging itself at will, my intentions strewn all over, like our clothes only moments before. *If Wongani was still here*, I told myself, *I would have the courage to speak my mind.* I sucked in air, but it was stabbing, as if I had been running.

Amama stopped my thoughts with a slap, dropping her hoe. "Shut up!" she spat. "Just shut up. What do you think you know? Zaka khumi ndizithatu, enh?" Only thirteen years old, she reminded me. "And those baby breasts have given you false courage. A child is never too old for its mother, Njemile. Me." She stabbed her chest. "I will bend you the right way!" Amama stalked off.

It turned out that there were worse things than the lash of Atata's leather.

The next morning, a wave of pain vibrated forward through my back and settled into a tight knot beneath my navel.

"What's wrong?" Amama asked, upon seeing my regular pauses between sweeping.

I clutched my stomach.

"Turn around."

When I did, Amama burst out in ululations, terrifying the chickens that had been pecking the ground. "Alalalalala!"

She yanked me into the hut and instructed me to unwrap the chitenge around my waist.

"Have you been with a man?" She was pacing but watching my eyes for a lie.

I scrunched up my nose. "No," I said. *No man.*

"Enh, keep it that way. Because if a man touches you, you will get pregnant."

My mind wandered to Wongani. Soft in every place, me melting between her legs into something slippery and milky.

"No man will touch me."

"No more school either."

A drop of blood landed on the rough floor.

"What do you mean?" I thought she would let me take the grade seven exams, at least.

"Which grown woman have you seen going to school?"

"I am not grown, Amama!" I protested.

The walls began to close in on me.

"Enhe, so now you know that you are not grown." She was ripping and folding my chitenge into neat squares. "And another thing. I don't want to see you climbing trees or running around pa nsaka."

"How am I supposed to pluck mangoes?"

She laughed a little. "Mangoes? My girl, any mango that is still in the tree is not yet ready to be eaten, but that leaking blood shows you are ripe. Soon, the mango will fall, and I have to make sure the right person is there to pick it." She handed me the pile of fabric and told me to place it between my underwear. "Use one and change it every hour, then wash the soiled one."

I nodded and watched her walk out.

After my first blood, Headman Amutengo came to talk to Atata underneath the mango tree. They chatted until the sun stole their shade while I served them trays of roasted mice and gourds of chipumu, Atata's favorite traditional beer.

The next evening, my marriage lessons started.

I learned that the string of rainbow-colored beads around my waist was for the wrinkly headman's amusement and not for "shaping" my midriff into the eight-shape of a soft drink bottle. I learned how to gyrate in bed to please my future husband. His pubic hair was to be razored off by me. I gasped at this, picturing the slivers of gray on his gleaming head. That gasp earned me a pinch between my thighs. Which brought us to the next lesson. By keeping a mouthful of water and rocks without a spill, I learned the importance of my silence in case the impending husband disciplined me with a beating.

The end of that wet season returned the vicious cold, and with it came my wedding day.

I awoke from a fitful sleep, half wishing the thatched roof would collapse and crush me, the other half excited about my future. Headman Amutengo's house was, after all, the only brick house in the village, with an indoor toilet. His wives did not go to the river with the rest of the women; his children were the only ones in the whole village with several pairs of shoes.

"Njemile," Amama said, pushing open the creaky metal door. "Kwacha. Uka."

I rubbed sleep from my eyes and squinted against the shards of light she was letting in behind her.

"As the youngest wife, you will need to rise early," she said, pulling my blanket off. "The headman paid a good bride price for you." Three heads of cattle to add to Atata's dying herd.

"Yes, Amama."

I strode out into the yard and memorized my home.

A flock of chickens, led by a sparsely feathered rooster, were pecking the ground nearby. Next to them, a dewy patch of grass where I had once molded mud into dolls, practiced plaiting on the weeds, and basked in the sun. To my left, my parents' hut appeared to stoop as they now did. Amama's chigugu, with its stew of aromas—steamed pumpkin leaves, boiled maize—sat next to that. I blinked at the ever-flourishing wild spinach next to the pit latrine.

A thought latched onto me and guided my feet softly toward the toilet behind my hut. Behind it, I careened into the field of overgrown grass and took the long way out of the village. At first, hesitating over broken sticks and sharp pebbles, then lurching through the shrubs as though a hyena were chasing me, I finally stumbled into the maize field that led to our inswa cave.

Alone on that rock, I weighed my options.

Staring at the vast grasslands, I imagined the Great East Road on the other side, flirted with the thought of escaping to Malawi in the east, or west, toward the year-old capital, Lusaka. But as quickly as the idea had come, it was replaced by the image of my mother's fate if I ran away: she would be banished at least or die of heartbreak at most. My father, reckless as he was with his words, worshipped my mother and would never let them run her out of the village. So this, I knew, could swiftly kill my mother.

But being on that rock kept Wongani's face as vivid as if she were smiling at me. And if I stayed here, it would kill me too.

"There you are!" Wongani exclaimed. "Your mother has been looking all over for you!"

I let my eyes wash over the mane of black hair that framed her flawless face. For a moment, I almost forgot my paralyzing fear.

"Why?" I asked.

"Why?" she mocked, folding her arms. "Why do you think? Are you not almost a wife?"

My eyes welled up.

"Hey," she softened, kneeling. "Relax. It's fine, eh. Don't worry." Her voice was low, eyes dancing.

"No. It's not okay!"

"Njemile. Come on." She grinned. "Give me inswa." She kissed my tears, walked her fingers over my breasts, paused to feel my racing heart, and smiled. Then she placed one nipple into her warm mouth and groaned like the sweetest juice spilled from it, straight into her soul.

"Let us run away." I was trying to sound steady.

She groaned into my chest, ignoring me.

My breath quickened. "We can do it, Wongani. Escape to the city. To Lusaka. Remember what the teacher said?"

She ran her fingers over my navel and into the sweaty patch between my legs, prodding the pea-sized bean amid a forest of curly black hair.

"Wongani." My voice demoted to a whisper.

One finger, two fingers, just the tip of three.

"Wongani."

The inswa spread to my back, my tongue and throat, coming out as a squeal I had been repressing since our first kiss.

Afterward, we lay on the ground, watching the sun dip west into the big city, while our breathing calmed.

Wongani stood and dusted herself off.

"Where are you going?"

"Home, of course."

"But we can leave, Wongani, the teacher said—"

"That girls don't have to drop out of school in grade seven in Lusaka, I know."

"Yes!" I cried.

She pinched the bridge of her nose and then said, "Look, don't be stupid. Those are foolish dreams for...for people like us," she spat, darting her eyes this way and that, everywhere except at me.

"I know," I said, gathering my clothes, "but no one knows us there."

"Exactly," she answered, tying her chitenge tighter around her slim waist. "This is home."

"We can try."

"Where will we live?"

"I don't—" My mouth dried up.

"What will we eat? You want us to be one of those women who paint their faces and wait for men in the street?"

"No." My ears started to buzz.

"Then what?" She shrugged. "You take things too serious, naiwe Njemile." Her words sucked the air from my lungs. "If you want to be a disgrace to your family, that's up to you. I'm going home." The flurry in my tummy ceased.

She gave me her back and disappeared into the field.

Wongani's way, turning the extraordinary into the mundane.

A flying termite zipped across my thigh.

I straightened my chitenge and turned west, into the setting sun. I knew exactly what to do.

A DOCTOR, A LAWYER, AN ENGINEER, OR A SHAME TO THE FAMILY

Mulendo ni nkhuku yituwa.
A stranger is a white hen.
—**Tumbuka proverb**

Dear Nanozga,

Per Amama's instruction, this letter should be something beautiful about what it means to be Zambian, from aunt to newborn niece. A fifteen-page gift for your future self from your naming ceremony.

From the videos my cousins in Zambia occasionally share on our WhatsApp family group—Banja—a proper ceremony would be held in the wealthiest relative's sitting room. Uncles would be reclined on leather sofas, sipping on sweating bottles of Mosi. Giggling children, listless drumming, and nostalgic kalindula music would all clamor to be heard over the aunties' joyful ululations.

In Zambia, Amama, your grandmother, would whisper your name.

Then she'd bless you by spitting onto your forehead and then slowly massaging her saliva into your pulsing fontanel.

Your actual naming ceremony, north of loud family gatherings and the equator, is taking place at my parents' town house in downtown Minneapolis. The living room is 1999 Lusaka, but for the frosty purr of the AC in the corner and the twenty-one years that have gifted us eye bags and drawn-out silences. All three thrifted couches are wearing crocheted white doilies—thin veils Amama stitched together to cover the stains that wouldn't budge, neither to the persistence of her scrubbing nor vinegar soaks.

My parents and yours, my two older brothers, and I are now congregated against the commotion of cushions arranged above the doilies. The younger half of the two generations are trading whispers to nudge the time along as we nurse fat coffee mugs filled with Coors Light. In truth, we're waiting for the politest time to mutter, "Well, we should do this again soon," which is Minnesotan for "I've socialized enough now, bye!"

Adada, your grandfather, is slurping his drink out of the *orld's B st Dad!* mug from several Father's Days ago, each noisy gulp making his tongue looser. At his elbow, Radio Christian Voice is streaming from the speaker sitting on a stool between him and Amama. My mother can't figure out how to reset the Wi-Fi password or find the temperature between searing and freezing on the thermostat, but somehow she manages to stream her favorite radio station from eight thousand miles away every single day.

When the last chords of Kirk Franklin's "Imagine Me" died out, Amama wound down the volume, hunched over your cradle, and kicked the ceremony off with, "Zina lako ndiwe Nanozga."

Startled, you extended your arms like maybe you'd let out one of your massive wails. But it's your mom, Masozi, who shifted in her spot, hovered over your bassinet a third—no, fourth time, with a wet film in her eyes. You instead curled back up, sucked your thumb, and continued sleeping quietly.

Your muted reaction to Amama's statement—"Your name is Nanozga"—meant the same thing here as it would've in those Banja videos; you had accepted your name.

Both your parents grinned, tasting the three syllables on their tongues, "Na-no-zya."

Amama chanted the meaning of the name into your downy head. "God has made everything beautiful, in his own time." She rose, spun around, and shot her jubilation at the ceiling with earsplitting ululations. But when a neighbor pounded, "Shut the fuck up!" through the thin wall, Amama stilled, tongue-to-roof-of-mouth, and sank back into the couch. She dug in the satchel she keeps beneath the side table and fished out a notepad. "Well," she declared, "I think we should all write Nanozga a letter, enh?"

Adada immediately objected. "A letter for what? The child is a fucking week old." He was past slurring, well into drunken swearing, on his way to stumbling, tripping over nothing, and crashing to the floor if he rose for another drink just one more time. "Kid prolly smells like hospital bleach if you lean in close enough." He belched, his expression the lick-of-freshly-sliced-lemon sour, then said, "Kidding, kidding."

Amama stuffed the ensuing silence with "I thought" and "maybe" and "wouldn't it be lovely if we just wrote her something beautiful, enh? About what it means to be Zambian."

"What it means to be Zambian," Adada scoffed. "And why must we write it? We all dying tomorrow or what? The child moving 'cross the goddamn oceans? No? Then we'll tell her our damn selves!"

"I just thought…" Her voice crumbled. "Since we can't do the ceremony properly—"

"Properly? That shit flew out the window the day your daughter decided to spread her legs."

The scorned daughter, your mother, leaped from her seat.

"No, that's a good idea, Amama. It'll help us all keep it down in here. She, I mean, Nanozga doesn't sleep very well at night." This placation Masozi whispered in the velvet sound that is her voice, an applause-arousing gift that earned her the lead in every musical all through high school.

And with that, Adada threw his arms into the air and offered Masozi his wonky smile.

"Good," Amama said, ripping out and handing us each a sheet of paper. "Then it is agreed. Remember. Something beautiful, enh? About what it really means to be Zambian."

A younger me, who could blame my sarcasm on the flaming hormones scalding my face with acne, would've swiftly pointed out the living room clock; a copper face shaped like the map of Zambia, and the fact that Amama is draped in a chitenge dress, whose flowers are the green, orange, black, and red of the Zambian flag. But twenty-eight-year-old Tiyo is as even-tempered as my Oxy-smooth skin. So I nodded along with everyone else at Amama's instruction.

I took a swig of my beer and Googled *What is Zambian culture?*

In approximately 1.33 seconds, 5,620,000 appeared. *Five million six hundred and twenty thousand!* That means, if you want to learn one of the seventy-two languages, plan trips around Zambia's twenty traditional ceremonies, or order yourself a 2012 AFCON-winning Chipolopolo T-shirt with NANOZGA etched at the back of the orange jerseys in 2036, you can do it without the help of any letter.

Amama—like she could read my mind—aimed her frown at me. *Something beautiful about our culture, enh* bitten along with her bottom lip as she turned Radio Christian Voice back up.

I didn't roll my eyes, didn't cry "What?" or complain about her always assuming the worst about me. See? Even-tempered. I am writing the letter, yes. But instead, I'll let you in on some Ndhlovu family culture. A cheat sheet for how to *not* disappoint your Zambian parents. At least not in the ways we do. Besides, we'll all seal these letters ourselves, and I can rest assured that you'll find your spit blessing intact in the one Amama is writing to you.

Caveat: I've refilled my mug a couple of times already, so excuse the handwriting.

1. Be born first (and male) AND MALE.

Amama's favorite lie is that she loves all four of us exactly the same, à la God of Romans 2:11. Her proof is our photos, framed in identical 8x12s, hanging on the wall next to the dining table. As if four pictures arranged in order of birth can erase three decades of naked favoritism.

Masozi and I came six years after Amama and Adada already had Lusubilo, their boy, to carry the Ndhlovu name, and five years after Chawanangwa, the spare. But in the small picture of our naming ceremony glued to the back page of a family album, Amama stares out from the glossy paper with big, depleted eyes. Masozi and I are the bundles of white cradled into the crook of her arms, the source of her exhaustion since January 1990. Beneath the picture, our twin names echo our parents' sentiments: Tiyowoyechi & Masozi—"What can we say? & Tears." Unlike the praises that mark my brothers' first photographs. Lusubilo. *Hope.* Chawanangwa. *Blessing.*

In Zambia, it hadn't mattered. Not as much, anyway.

But after they hauled us to America, there was no sweet, wet dirt aroma to mask the smell of eggs and bacon while Masozi and I yawned awake. No squawking chickens in the backyard to offset the crackle of grease bubbles in a frying pan at dawn. Sure, Amama scrubbed the evidence off their plates and offered us two slices of toast in its place, but the porky stench betrayed her every time. It crept into the threads of her chitenge wrapper like a secret and settled there. So, when I reached up to hug her *good morning,* I was wrapped in the aroma of her lotion lingering with bacon fat.

"Women, Tiyo," Amama told me the one time I questioned her on it, "should not eat pork. Bad for your womb and worse for your skin." And that was that.

You won't have that problem, though. Even though Amama was all kissed teeth and "You know what children are like, they don't listen. They do whatever they want" to her church friends about Masozi's pregnancy, she now can't stop telling us how "Bazukulu bakunowa kulusya bana."

Grandchildren must indeed be *sweeter than children* because Adada grows so soft whenever he holds you, his frown lines near fading at the mere sight of your face.

I know you're here on purpose because I was the one who found the unopened strip of birth control pills in Masozi's cabinet months before her stomach swelled, the one who held her hand the entire five minutes it took for the two lines to stain the white pregnancy test pink. Before I could offer up solutions, tell her it would be fine, Masozi's cheeks dimpled, she flashed me a smile, and I knew.

Your birth is not like ours, the first disappointment.

2. Become a doctor.

Your Uncle Lusubilo fulfilled his fated role as the first son of immigrant parents by getting accepted into pre-med. Amama and Adada already called him Doc, the way other parents might shorten a name. Every twenty-ninth of April, Amama piped *Happy Birthday Doc* onto Lusubilo's coffee cake. So, of course she made him wear his bone-white Dominican University T-shirt the entire week before his first semester and paraded him on all her errands. Of course the whole family crammed into the battered Sienna for the ten-hour drive that could've been seven, max, if Adada didn't insist on crawling at fifty miles per hour on the I-94 "to save gas."

It was 10:00 p.m. by the time we delivered Lusubilo safely to his dormitory, a nondescript gray building tucked between pristine lawns. On the paved walkways bathed with white light, the four of us children posed for a photo. Afterward, Amama mailed a copy of our washed-out faces to every family member with a PO box in Zambia. **DR. LUSUBILO SAMUEL NDHLOVU'S FIRST DAY OF MEDICAL SCHOOL!** announced her note.

Instead of graduating—instead of brandishing his stethoscope for our parents' friends during Sunday lunches and reassuring Amama that *no*, her dizzy spells were not because of low blood pressure, she just didn't eat enough protein—Lusubilo dropped out. To become a writer, of all things, which was not on the list of expected professions.

"You're doing what?" Adada's voice shook into the phone when Lusubilo made the call.

I picked up the hallway handset as Adada was screaming, "Doctors write, Lusubilo! Don't doctors write? Doctors write useful things. Like prescriptions and medical books! What is this foolishness about wanting to be a writer? Better stop with this fucking nonsense!"

A choked silence met Adada's rage while Amama said, "Oh my God," again and again. I didn't realize I was pacing in circles until I had wound the telephone cord around my waist, inwardly begging Lusubilo, *Answer them, answer them.*

But silence is Lusubilo's confidence.

Uncertain, he might have stammered, "P-p-please," but thirty long seconds later, he was still quiet.

When Adada finally spoke again, his Tumbuka was carefully enunciated. "Upulikenge," he said. As if by demanding *Listen to me* in Tumbuka rather than English, Lusubilo would remember himself—the obedient firstborn Zambian son. "You'll stop this foolishness right now. We didn't come all the way to this country—we didn't make so many sacrifices—just for you to throw it all away!"

More silence.

Amama chimed in to beg then. "Doc," she said. "What about my blood pressure? You know these doctors here don't take my distress seriously. You are my only Hope," she said. Her last resort—reminding Lusubilo of the meaning of his name.

Usually, Lusubilo would agree. He'd placate her with "You're right, Amama," arms hanging limply by his sides, caterpillar eyebrows in a bunch. But in the safety of distance, Lusubilo replied, "But this makes me happy, Amama. You do want me to be happy, right?"

It was their turn to be quiet.

"Lord, what have I done to deserve this?" Amama croaked.

Slowly, I unwound myself from the cord, pulled the phone away from my ears, and gently replaced it against the magnetic black button so they wouldn't hear me hang up as Lusubilo's silence was supplanted by the dial tone.

That was the second disappointment.

3. Become a lawyer.

To Chawanangwa's credit, he, at least, graduated from law school and as valedictorian too. Amama ordered doubles of his commencement pictures from CVS so that she could mail them to Zambia through FedEx. Three weeks via USPS simply would not do. **ATTORNEY CHAWANANGWA NDHLOVU!** penned in Amama's crisp block letters on the back of each photograph, in case it wasn't clear without the white wig and bib, which lawyers donned back home.

Amama didn't have to wait for Chawanangwa to pass his bar exams, for her to sniffle "My son" and "Thank you, Jesus," while Chawanangwa swore to "support the Constitution of the United States and that of the state of Minnesota, and conduct himself as an attorney and counselor at law in an upright and courteous manner, to the best of his learning and ability." So help him, God.

But then, right after Chawanangwa's admission to the bar, before Amama had the chance to call her sisters in Zambia and beam into the phone about how proud she was of him, Chawanangwa proposed to the white woman he'd met while volunteering for Meals on Wheels. Amama still calls her this after all these years. *The Meals on Wheels Woman*. Even after Chawanangwa had explained that Morgan was a doctor, even after he rattled out her CV to Amama like Morgan was interviewing for a job in the family. His go-to asterisk on her long list of accomplishments being "She was a Fulbrighter too, Amama. Did I tell you?"

He had.

Amama ignored him. Assaulting him instead with statements like, "Morgan is a man's name," and "You do want a wife, not a husband, don't you?" and "You know white women make their husbands cook? And with a name like that, well, you'll be cleaning and doing all the laundry too."

When he said nothing in reply, Amama took it upon herself to settle her feelings about Morgan not being African (criteria number one) or at least Black (the second acceptable qualification) by asking Chawanangwa's former Fulbrighter, medical doctor fiancée if she'd at least be taking the family name after the wedding. Which wouldn't have been as bad had Amama not chosen to do it between the appetizers and main dish at the rehearsal dinner.

Morgan speared what was left of her smoked salmon and lifted it to her mouth. She chewed on the morsel so slowly that Masozi blurted, "Morgan, did you know, *Ndhlovu* means 'Elephant'!"

Laughter rippled across the table as metal scraped against ceramic plates, the moment apparently swallowed by Masozi's reaction to the awkwardness.

Banter returned, but the bride-to-be and Amama eyed each other with tight smiles from opposite ends of the long table.

"No," Morgan announced finally.

Chawanangwa coughed and concentrated on his napkin, arranged into the shape of an angular rose.

"Your son didn't go to medical school," Morgan clipped. "I did."

She meant Chawanangwa, of course, but Amama clasped that insult as tight as a rosary to her chest. So, although Amama and Adada attended the one-hundred-and-fifty-guest wedding the following evening at Hutton House and grinned for the pictures against the all-white rose backdrop, Amama never let that slight go.

That was the third disappointment.

4. Become (or marry) an engineer.

By tenth grade, our parents knew Masozi would not become the engineer they hoped for. Masozi was undeterred by the *Why can't you be more like your sister?* sermons, which Amama delivered every time Masozi brought home another litany of C's. But as the girl with those billboard jewelry-ad fingers, R&B video hips, and skin the shade that Amama warned her to keep out of the sun, I think our mother's comfort was that Masozi could at least marry one.

Masozi met Ian the day Adada finally admitted that he couldn't fix the microwave without sparks flying everywhere and called the only Zambian handyman within fifty miles of home. He arrived in a navy work suit, which Masozi remarked "fit him like a glove" afterward.

Six months later, when Adada said, "Ask your daughter why the hell she's wearing winter clothes in summer?"

Amama replied simply, "The devil entered these children, and they're now trying to kill me one by one." Even though it was apparent from Masozi's swollen face, blackened neck, loud retching into the toilet, and her sudden insatiable taste for anchovy sandwiches, why Masozi had traded her tight tank tops for my roomy hoodies.

After that, neither Amama nor Adada talked to Masozi until I sent the "The baby is here ♀!" text to Banja with a photo of you swaddled in the green-and-pink hospital blanket.

An hour later, our parents bustled into the maternity wing at Abbott Northwestern. They were encircled in a cloud of pink balloons, all *God is good, all the time*, in lieu of congratulations.

But that fuss is almost over now. Your cord stump has fallen off, which is the only time it's proper to name you. (Hey, I snuck in some Zambian culture after all!)

Yesterday, Ian popped the question with a small sapphire. After an appropriate amount of sobbing and mouth-smacking, Masozi gushed, "A million times yes!" and shoved her left hand in his face.

Amama could finally exhale. In the letters she will post to Zambia, I bet she'll say Ian is an engineer.

But there'll be no reception with deafening kalindula blaring through the mounted speakers—a missed opportunity for my parents to put their new American success on display.

Adada grimaced when Masozi told him that she would be taking Ian's name. Moyo, it seems, was a good enough surname to fix the microwave and prevent a small kitchen fire, but not good enough for his youngest daughter.

That was the fourth disappointment.

5. Or a shame to the family.

In a month, I'll graduate with an SJD. My thesis is called *The Marriage Between Secret-Keeping and Social Justice in Zambia*. My parents are finally getting their doctor, even if it's in law. But in Amama's eyes, I'm forever sixteen, splayed on my bed that day she swung my door open.

In my recollection of it, her "Tiyo?" is crushed in with my "God!" as I thrust my hips into my best friend Mei's mouth. Amama squeezed her eyelids shut as if shoving the image out of her mind and said, "Tiyo-woyechi. I'll count to three. When I open my eyes, that demon better be gone."

Those three beats, punctuated by Amama raising one slim finger after another, were the shortest countdown of my life. I swallowed hard, yanked the sheet above my breasts, and glanced around the room I shared with Masozi. I felt sure that this would be the last time I saw our twin beds, the massive poster of Justin Timberlake hanging above hers, and the framed RBG quote that hung above mine. Irrationally, I read it like a goodbye to the room while Mei scrambled out of the sheets, pulled her shirt on, and slipped into her sneakers—*My mother told me to be a lady. And for her, that meant be your own person, be independent.*

The *demon* escaped through my bedroom window after murmuring, "Catch ya later, T."

When her feet slammed the sidewalk below, Amama opened her eyes. She blinked, unveiling that depleted look from the baby photo as if just the sight of me sapped all the energy from her.

"Tiyowoyechi," Amama said wearily. The meaning of my name imbued in her breathless whisper. *What can I say?*

My tongue went limp, lead-heavy with the weight of unspoken words.

"Where—When—?" She grows breathless.

My words refused to come.

"Start talking," she said. "Before your father gets home."

I glanced at the open window, but I remained glued between sheet and duvet, immobile, while Amama glared at me. On one side of whatever answer I offered would be Adada summoning me to the living room, flogging my back with his belt until the skin burst and wept red. On the other side was Amama dragging me with her to church, splashing holy water into my hair, letting her tears and sweat drip onto my face while she prayed the evil out of me at the foot of a wooden altar, *In Jesus's mighty name, amen.*

I weighed these options for a split second, searching the criss-crossing lines that slithered over my open palms for a solution.

"Tiyowoyechi Ndhlovu!"

I picked the second.

"From the magazines in Adada's box in the storage closet," I whispered.

Amama's gaze snaked over me, brimming with disgust. "What did you say?"

"It's true, I swear! He keeps them in the green toy box labeled 'taxes.' Beneath last year's returns and Lusubilo's old textbooks."

I might have been too old for Amama to squeeze the flesh of my thighs, but no one was above one of her biting slaps. While I braced myself for it, she stood there, shaking my words out of her head.

"If—" she started to say, but then suddenly she spun out of the room.

In her wake came stomping down the stairs, a key fighting a lock, a door squeaking open, metal clanging against linoleum tiles, a plastic tub clicking open, papers shuffling, magazine pages tearing apart, a gasp, a door slamming, and then more stomping approaching my door.

I expected her to accuse me of stashing them there myself. I was ready for her admonition—*How dare you accuse your own father shamelessly?* But when Amama returned, she stood at my door for a long moment without uttering a word.

"Amama—"

She raised a hand, stalked the length of my bed until she was glowering over me. "Upulikenge," she said. "We will never speak about this again."

I nodded.

When she left, I puffed out air—a forced exhale to summon relief that would never come because to Amama, the *this* was me: the fifth disappointment.

In Zambia, your ceremony would end like every other party: a few hours after the aunties have said "We should really be going now, it's so late" and done nothing about it, long after the cousins have slid themselves under the covers with a favorite cousin, and all the uncles are long past the legally permitted blood alcohol concentration. Laughter and dust clouds would trail each departing vehicle, promises of future visits lifting into the night air.

Here, the letters are almost completed. Amama is collecting them like test papers, without asking us any questions. Panic sheathes itself around my neck in wild wonder as I finish mine. *Will Amama open them and read them aloud?*

Instead, each folded paper Amama takes, she hands to your mother and says, "Give them to Nanozga on her sixteenth birthday, enh?"

In turn, we nod, smile, and reply, "We should do this again soon."

Love, love, love,
Aunt Tiyo

REFLECTIONS

Umoyo ni usambazi.
Life is wealth.
—Tumbuka proverb

Mummy was fanning herself on the sofa, busy yelling at the Africa Magic channel while I rummaged through her musty closet. I could've been nestled in the avocado tree, twisting a wheel for my latest wire car. But Mummy had this habit of sending me on useless errands, like fetching her dowdy yellow sweater even though it was the middle of August and melting hot. I scanned the tight space once more and groaned, "I can't find it."

The TV volume slid down, sofa springs creaked, and Mummy snapped back at me in her native tongue, "Iwe, Ngale, if I come in there and find it myself, wapya!"—threats. The "you'll see" jolted me up, straight into one of Daddy's trouser legs suspended on a plastic hanger. I tugged on them, wicked in Daddy's essence—Brut aftershave and Stuyvesant cigarettes—as the soft fabric fell and pooled around my skinned ankles. A belt was still hooked to one of the trouser loops. I lifted it, wrapped it around my waist twice, and smiled.

"Ngale?"

I rolled my eyes and tried to unlatch the belt. "I'm coming." But it wouldn't budge.

"Has the thing locked itself again?" Mummy asked.

I tumbled out of the wardrobe onto the polished bedroom floor and fought with the buckle again, but the clip above my navel refused to move. I imagined what Mummy might say: *You couldn't find what I sent you for, and yet there you are, standing in your father's trousers, eh?* And my mouth went dry. "Yes?" I whined back.

Mummy nudged the door again. *Click.* "Well." *Click.* "Girl." *Click.* "Open." *Click.* "It!" Each snap of the door latch cut the air from my throat, pressing the brick walls into me while everything else stayed still. Leather belt, Mukwa wooden door, me—fixated on the word *girl*. Mummy flung it into every conversation as if merely saying it would make it true.

"Don't call me that!" I spat back, smacking my mouth too late.

"Chani?"

I knew better than to repeat myself, and I darted my gaze around the room. Each item my eyes landed on morphed into a weapon: shoes piled high on the rack, belts hanging from a bent nail in the wall, all waiting for Mummy to grab and flog me.

Mummy sucked her teeth. "Use the scissors on the dresser to open it. *Now.*"

I could already picture her ripping through her chitenge wrapper to kick the door in and drag me out. My stomach clenched, and I inched away. Instead, she said, "Girl," in a whisper begging to be a window-shattering scream, "Ngale, you better open this door right now."

She was going to flog me no matter what. Tell me how when she was my age, she had never disrespected her mother. How she was not going to raise an insolent child because the world would just blame her. I might as well stay inside for as long as I could, protect my skin from being licked into obedience. "No," I said.

A long moment snaked past, stuffing the room with a heavy silence, until Mummy said, "If you'll stay in there forever, then it's fine," and stormed off. Each flap of her flip-flops on the floor pushed the walls back into place, my ears popped, and sounds streamed in through the open window above my parents' bed: a sprinkler hissing into the grass, dogs barking in the distance, and the fluttering of avocado leaves. I turned to the mirror, where a dusty-faced girl blinked back.

Mummy often said that staring at my reflection too long would make me cross-eyed. The girl in the mirror snorted abruptly, then yanked the two silver studs out of her earlobes. She winced, ripped off her lacy green blouse, and pulled out the polka-dot bow crowning the kinky puff piled on top of her head. Panting, she shook her coils loose, grabbed the scissors, and slashed her hair until a boy emerged, eyes wet, cropped hair, white vest, oversize trousers knotted around a narrow waist, grinning: me. Just then, a car revved at the gate. As the rusty metal squeaked open, my stomach clenched a little. Past the singing crickets in the flowering hibiscus hedge, a yellow Accord hobbled over the rubble and parked outside the bedroom window. The driver's door swung open.

I squealed. "Daddy!"

"Mwana wanga," he answered, and I felt a smile warm my core with his endearment.

I wobbled toward the door.

"Let me in, please?" Daddy asked a few moments later.

"It's stuck."

He coughed. "Will you step back, then?"

I did, beaming as the door swung in after one thud. The bulb in the corridor cloaked him in a white glow as he crouched in, all rumpled clothes, wrinkled face, and a smile twinning mine. He knelt for me to wrap my arms around his neck and kiss him on the cheek. His stubble tasted like black pepper and sweat.

"This daughter of yours," Mummy exploded into the corridor from the kitchen. "She's been locked in there all afternoon doing God knows what!"

Daddy peeled away from me, placed one hand on his chest, and sighed. "Did you try opening it?"

That's when Mummy saw me and screamed. "What have you done to your hair?!"

I cowered behind Daddy's briefcase.

"Wicked!" Mummy screeched. "Wicked, wicked child."

Daddy frowned. "But it's just hair. Won't it grow back?"

Mummy flitted past us, ignoring the synthetic wig slipping from her head as she bent to gather my hair from the floor into balls. "Just hair, eh! Like her tree climbing is just a habit?" She spun back and narrowed her eyes at me. "Now listen to me, girl." She pulled down on her earlobe, as she'd have done to mine if Daddy wasn't there. "If you don't stop with all this nonsense, one day those boys you call friends will stick something between those legs! And—"

My eyes widened. *And?*

But Daddy cut her off with a slap of his yellowed hand across her face.

I flinched, reliving the moment he'd slapped me for placing fourth instead of first in the last term of grade two. My palms moistened; I backed into the wall and whimpered.

Mummy and Daddy had fought before, shot hot, ugly words behind the veil of their bedroom wall, but this was the first time I'd seen any part of their bodies touch.

The creases on Daddy's forehead smoothened. "None of that, mwana wanga," he soothed, bumping past Mummy to take my hand.

With my hair still in her hands, Mummy slumped into the bed, and our eyes locked in the mirror, hers glistening with tears, and I wished I could re-attach my hair if it would only bring back her voice. But then she blinked, scrunched the ball of fuzz between her fingers, and tossed it into the bin at the foot of their bed.

In the weeks that followed, Mummy clutched her silence as tightly as a purse filled with money until my hair grew just long enough for her to say, "Come here, nkuluke." I planted myself on a cushion between her legs and closed my eyes while she twisted three-stranded fikuti into my hair. Mummy had called my hair a crowning glory; she'd stretched it with a white-hot metal comb straight off the brazier, tucked it into long synthetic braids, and lathered the roots with Blue Magic grease, but never before had she used it as a weapon. So I bit my lip as she pulled my edges and waited for the next morning. While Mummy washed our laundry under the outside tap, I sneaked out of the yard and ran to the tin metal barbershop near Woodlands Shopping Complex, where Daddy cut his hair every other weekend.

"I'm shaving it off," I announced to the barber, who was sweeping hair into a pile in the corner.

He stopped. "What?"

"Like that," I replied, pointing at a poster of a bald man.

"But you have such lovely hair," he protested.

I patted the tiny braids the way Mummy would when I aired my school shoes outside or took the plates into the kitchen after dinner. "The time is eight ten on QFM," announced a dusty black radio in the corner. I wavered, catching my reflection in his mirror. If I ran back home right then, Mummy wouldn't even know I'd left. It would be as if I'd just crawled up the avocado tree again to bend bits of wire into toys. But I knew she'd find me and say something like, "Why can't you just make mud dolls like other girls?"

No, I decided, propping myself in the barber's chair. "Make it as smooth as this," I said, showing him my arm.

"Money first," he said, stretching out his palm.

Finally, I could put the loose change Mummy let me keep after buying tomatoes to use.

"Yes." I handed him five crumpled two-kwacha notes and swathed myself in one of his threadbare towels.

"You'd look just like your father's son if not for that skirt," the barber said to me when he was done. I ran my hand over my head and smiled at the sensation—*my father's son*. I felt as light as the air.

I skipped back home, outrunning the children that sniggered "girl-boy" at me as I slipped between the straight line of houses leading to mine and slinked into our yard through the itchy shrubs. Clean clothes were swinging on the line, and Mummy was humming in the kitchen. I lingered on the veranda until the aromas of her paprika chicken stew drew me slowly in.

"Mwelesa!" she cried, dropping her cooking stick. *Dear God!* She snatched it back up and lashed me with it until she was breathless. "What did I do to deserve such an insolent child?"

That's the Mummy I remember now as I scowl at the bathroom mirror, binding my breasts with a pair of worn tights, choking back tears as I wrap a chitenge around my pants. I squeeze myself into the white T-shirt with Daddy's face across the front and squint at the words etched across:

REDFORD MWANZA
12/07/63–17/09/11
Revelation 21:4

I'm glaring at the string of foul letters and numbers when someone knocks on the door.

"What?"

"Mwana wanga, we have to go now," Mummy says.

I stiffen and ball my fingers into a fist, ready to unravel them and scratch the words from her tongue. *Mwana wanga.* How dare she say it now? Taint Daddy's voice with her shrill one? I spin around, unlock the door, and glare at her. But the Mummy who looks in, eyes brimmed red, head covered in a black chitambala, is not the one who had forced me into this costume. "Don't call me that." It comes out wobbly, like my legs. I grip the door-frame.

"If you don't come now, the cars will leave," Mummy murmurs.

I kick a chipped floor tile and trail her into the sitting room. If I shut my eyes, I can pretend Daddy is still on the sofa, tapping his cigarette butt into an ashtray and swearing at the news. I can almost unsee the line of mattresses lying side by side on the carpet instead of four corduroy couches as I wade outside. Last night's fire is dying underneath an army-green tent pitched above the patch of grass where Daddy taught me how to ride my bike when I was five. I step into Elm Road, lined with cars on both sides, and inch my way to the one assigned to Mummy and me.

I slump in beside her and stare at the back of the headrest while the car purrs on. We roll onto Woodlands' streets dotted with memories of Daddy. Through my tinted window, the echoes of him reel past with the tree trunks: me, aged ten, waiting for Daddy outside G Club at our street corner, where he gave me my first swig of Mosi beer; past the barbershop where we'd been shaving our heads every second Saturday of the month since I was eight; stopping at St. Andrew's Church, where Daddy brought me once aged twelve after Mummy left for her parents' village and swore on her dead mother's grave to never return. Now Daddy's been reduced to a two-paged tribute being handed out by Aunt Hazel at the steps of the church. She trots to meet us. "Here," she says breathlessly, shoving a chitenge into me. I glance down and see Daddy's pants clinging to my thighs.

My chest tightens as I examine Mummy's face and prepare my defense. The neat lines of frangipani trees fencing the church off from the road suddenly feel too close; I wipe my slick palms on my trousers. My chitenge must have slipped off as I was getting out of the car. But then Mummy croaks, "Please, leave her," and my mouth drops.

"I understand, mulamu," Daddy's sister whispers to Mummy, darting her eyes everywhere but me. "We're all grieving, but this is a house of God. She can't go in dressed like, well, like that." Aunt Hazel whispers the last word even though the other mourners are already staring.

Mummy straightens her shoulders. "Or what?"

Auntie Hazel folds her arms and narrows her eyes.

"He didn't care then about his dressing, and he won't care now."

There is a hardness to Mummy's voice, a steadiness in her face as she says this. And it is the surety in the three-letter word she has never allowed herself to say, in relation to me, that lets my body slump into hers. Mummy pulls me into her body, which is the opposite of her words. Her skin feels like home, familiar and soft.

Together we lumber into the massive, stained-glass-windowed building. The benches are crammed with people clicking their phones, but even the light tapping dies as Mummy and I walk past, leaving only the screeching microphone at the podium waiting for the reverend to speak. I tune him out when he does and focus on the photo of Daddy, which only four days ago hung on the sitting room wall but is now pitched on top of his coffin. I memorize the lines on his forehead, the V where his eyebrows meet, the crows out of the corners of his eyes, and his wonky smile over and over so that I'll remember him as he was in that picture: perfect. When the service is over, six grim pallbearers roll the coffin to the church door followed by pew after pew of mourners rising to peer into it, wail, dab their eyes, and then snap out into the sunshine as if they did not just see Daddy for the last time.

Eventually, Mummy and I follow.

Daddy's supposed to be tucked between the silk sheets of a gleaming white box. But the thing there, tiny cancer-eaten gray face sleeping behind the glass, isn't him. "That is not my father."

"Be strong," Mummy says, rubbing my back.

I shake her off. "Look!" His nose is pinched, black lips burnt pink, and body collapsed into itself so that everything is too large on him, white shirt, striped tie, and hands placed above his chest. "That—that is not my father," I stammer in between short breaths.

Mummy leans into me. I jerk back, catching a whiff of nicotine, but it's only one of Daddy's scarves draped loosely around her neck. "I know, mwana wanga," Mummy mutters, dissolving finally into sobs.

"DO NOT HATE ME."

Nchironda cha mkati chapalawo ungasinga.
It is an internal sore; an external one can be cleaned.

—Tumbuka proverb

once upon a night, We came to Msanide in his sleep.

that day's migraine had descended with the sun, then refused to ebb despite his mother's usual solutions.

—nsima,

—a blackened room,

—two crushed tablets of Panadol washed down with cool water,

—a prayer,

—and finally, a bedtime fairy tale to trick peace into coming.

"But Msanide sees us, doesn't he?"

even though his pupils are fixed on the thatched-grass fence behind us?

"He must."

even though he's in the same trance that seizes him each time the vibrations behind his eyeballs spread their fingers around his skull, down his neck, and squeeze?

"Surely, the boy can hear his own voices."

how can he not? We speak in the cracks of his great-grandmother's laughter; every breath between words comes from the way all of his dead aunties' sentences still crash into each other, cascade into his own past cries and the whispers of almost-formed siblings reabsorbed into the lining of his mother's womb, all of us woven into ancestors like freshly plaited mukule throbbing on a scalp.

"You'd think."

so, although We find his mind suffocated with flimsy things like *Will Chipolopolo beat Bafana Bafana?* already planning tomorrow's post-pain escape—through the glassless toilet window, leaping over blooming periwinkle weeds, twisting himself with the long, winding lanes of leaning bungalows that spill into Chisokone Market; We call him by the meaning of his name.

"Do not hate me." once.

but Msanide's mind is already in tomorrow's body, perched between stools, glued to the match on the neighborhood color TV, muting out the jeering men and their clinking beer bottles, already tracking the football flitting across the screen. "Wele! It's a goal." and his sleeping feet are already kicking his mother's shins.

"Do not hate me." twice.

storing our warning doesn't occur to him any more than other night-time things, like wet underpants or his baby brother Kachila's snoring stealing into his slumber.

so, this Msanide remains enjambed between the lingering sweetness of his mother's sweat and the smog that descends on him every time he closes his eyes.

and in this lifetime, he will always misname us *dream*.

the second time is nine years later. Msanide is now eighteen and the height of a door. We find him reeling from last night's hip-hop-induced gyrations at the Secondary School Leavers Ball. shots of Jameson are still coursing in his blood, so it takes a moment between his hands being suddenly empty and the smash of glass against skull for his world to simmer to silence.

he shuts out the scene in front of him and spots us between the splattering of red on the wall above Senior's deflating body.

"I'd only been trying to make him stop crying," he whimpers. "Senior never stops crying these days." which is to say, Msanide hadn't expected a thing as small as a vase to overpower the force of a man his father was. *Maybe he's just fainted?* Msanide thinks, even as the red seeps from Senior's last heaves.

to this Msanide, our voice is the gust of wind tornadoing around the bedroom as neighbors bang on the kitchen door. "Junior? Isulako! We heard screaming. Is everybody okay?" their usual questions and demands.

a soft pop of bubbles mark where the pool of blood ends.

"Do not hate me." once.

Msanide's feet stay bolted between the doorframe, fear blazing in his eyes. his father's spirit ascends to join us, and We ululate our welcome.

"Do not hate me." twice.

the neighbors succeed, and the kitchen door crashes to the floor.

Msanide's eyes flutter open.

women mill in first. they don't whisper "Careful," or "what is it this time?" but their steps are tentative, eyes darting everywhere. they're curious, not foolish. quietly, they collect the ingredients for their gossip soup—shards of glass, Senior's desolate stare, and the oozing, glass-embedded cut on his forehead. later, when the journalists come, these same neighbors will say how they found both Msanides screaming, the younger hovering over the older, smashing beer bottles? ashtrays? a DVD player? into Senior's face. right now, though, they gasp, "Mwe Lesa!" but their god does not answer.

phones are extracted from bras and chitenges. photos are snapped and posted with crying emojis, and enough frantic 999 calls giving the same Kitwe address soon attract sirens howling in the distance.

the issue We are excavating today lives between '91 and now, with Msanide's cramped memories of the mazed Wusakile streets.
—with the cast around his fractured arm in grade five,
—or vomiting after gorging on too much buttercream and not enough thirteenth birthday chocolate cake,
—and a rapturous joy-filled groan at the end of learning what his fingers, firm around his pulsing penis, could do the night after a boy first kissed him on the mouth.

last week, in a dim courtroom, a magistrate slammed her gavel against her podium. she tossed words at the suited lawyers standing in front of Msanide, like "juvenile offender" and "Msanide Jacob Phiri Junior" and "Eighth of November 2008" and "murder" and "Msanide Jacob Phiri Senior" and "Plea?"

"Insanity," one of the lawyers named us afterward, and police officers led Msanide to their van, drove him the five hours to Chainama for this medical determination.

now, with each day in this wretched hospital, each new matted-haired arrival and that relentless meow-like weeping at night, Msanide takes that word *insanity* and wears it, lets it cling to him like his hospital gown.

a doctor is meeting him in a room two doors from ward C. "I'm Dr. Chali," she says. "Remember me?"

Msanide finds the soft contours of Dr. Chali's cheeks, her dreadlocks piled into a ponytail in the middle of her head, and the gloved hands which had written his prescription for Fluoxetine and Diazepam. he nods.

"Good," she smiles. *all* she wants now is to understand how Msanide's father died, she tells him.

he blinks back, silent.

she shifts under his unwavering gaze, taps the file and says, "You do seem better."

Msanide leans over himself. he lifts a red fidget slug from the pile on the coffee table between them and twists its guts out. the slug's thick, pink, bumps could be his own pill-stained insides. he exposes them to her and watches her fingers flinch around her pen. the tip stabs a hole through the page, so she has to tug to snatch it out. in a faraway corner of his mind, We cackle.

"Better than what?"

Msanide smirks.

here, her voice drops to a feather. "Okay, let's try another way. What *can* you remember?"

it sounds like the name of a game he played as a child.

but how to explain that the last crisp thing in his mind remained on the floor of his mother's bedroom an almost decade ago?

"You can just start from the beginning," she nudges, "tell me why you think you're here?" Dr. Chali gestures at the whipping ceiling fan, dirty windows veiled with metal bars, the closed door, a bunch of keys dangling from a chain around her left wrist.

"Beginning?" Msanide asks.

"Is his life a story she's snuggled into her mama's bed to hear?"

or how exactly to explain blinking through the haze of sleep, locating the proof of it being a dream by telling himself, "Ona, Msanide—"?

"Yes!"

"I dreamt it," he explains, "when I was nine. That's how I knew how they'd die."

> We itch at the word *dream* and bicker among ourselves
> but don't fight him.

the doctor's penciled brows shoot up. "This is new," she whispers, "a dream, you say?"

"I mean," he shrugs, "Just that morning, the pawpaw tree was pregnant with the slow yellowing triplets of Ma's favorite sweet course, you see. It's only in dreams that they could've, in the blink of a day, turned the color of the sun in October, ready to drop any time, right? And in the trunk's endless shadow, Ma's chibwabwa garden mirrored the stars with its sweet blooms. Those four pumpkins had ballooned to twice their size overnight. Awake, wouldn't Ma have asked me to pluck one for her to cook in milk and douse with sugar for Kachila and me to eat already?"

all this, and she only writes *Schizophrenia?* underlining it twice in red.

> "Not a dream, but We saw it all too."

the way Msanide glanced over at the fruitless guava tree. the way memory flung him to Senior chopping it into the shape of a bike just for him the day before he left them. how, every day since that flight, Msanide had been unable to suspend his belief and see the severed branches as handlebars without also hearing Senior's axe against wood and picturing his father slicing through bark and Msanide's body all at once.

yet there it had stood to Msanide's left, erect again, bark glistening like the snakeskin of its future self when the tree would resprout branches.

"I mean, even Buyu—" Msanide continues.

"Buyu?"

"My cat's name. She should have been sleeping underneath our bed. But she lay in the crook of the guava tree." he smiles at the warmth of the memory of his white cat's breathing mimicking a dandelion in the wind.

Dr. Chali scratches off ~~Buyu~~, and replaces it with *cat*. "What else happened in this *dream*?"

Msanide snaps the guts back and tosses the fidget slug onto the wobbling pile.

she sighs. "If you just help me understand what happened—what happened to your father—then, then you'll be free."

"I always knew when they would die."

Dr. Chali keeps her back straight, but her breath quickens, and her lips shake as she says, "You knew when *and* how? How did you *know* exactly?" the last word peels off her mouth like a scab.

"I saw it."

"Good," We chorus. now he's remembering.

"Saw?"

"heard it too."

"Good boy."

"It?"

"Yes!"

"Yes."

"What did it say?"

in the language of proverbs, once more, we remind him.

"Do not hate me.
Calamity does not warn.
But what enters the ear stays for good.
Do not hate me.
On your unlucky day, even cold food will burn you.
This is how the tree falls to the ground, but the earth feels its pain."

the last chant belongs to the owner of the death day, so We grow still
as Msanide's baby brother chants

"So, mark the seventh of July."

then Msanide's mother

"mark the eighth of November."

Msanide grows sour, but he manages his own, "Eighth of November—"

"Yes," We agree.

nine-year-old Msanide's voice had retreated into toddlerhood. "Which year?" he'd muttered.

"But when you have no eyes, ears become eyes."

so, in the order of their demise, We poured his kin's faces into holes of flames in the fence.

the "Which year?" that followed was folded into a whisper. he hadn't even considered his annoyance of a little brother. he was so used to Kachila's footsteps chasing his when Msanide took his wire car out to play. as far back as the fingers of his memory could reach, the width of his own footsteps too wide for Kachila to ever catch up with him because in each recollection, before Msanide turned the first corner, Kachila hurled himself at the dirt, screaming for their mother.

so, *dream*, even as understanding latched into Msanide and the night air stilted. "Please," he said, still failing to visualize what a severing from Kachila might be.

dream. even though his mother's future, "My baby. God. My baby." scratched his present. "Please, when?"

dream. though he knew, the way a person knows themselves in a mirror.

"I just knew," Msanide says.

"Knew what?"

that his mother would never let Kachila go without following him the way she did when he toddled after Msanide. she'd always want to scoop him up, toss him onto her back and wrap him in a chitenge as if he was a baby still and not a toddler dangling his legs trying to shake free around her waist.

"Which year?" he'd repeated.

impatience rose inside us. "Wrong question."

the land shivered.

but *dream* because, after all, couldn't his mind's eye still see his mother turning the key in the kitchen door?

—weren't those her grunts echoing in his ears?

—couldn't he still see sweat pearling across her forehead as she lifted the burglar bars and hooked them into the two loops in the doorframe while Msanide reinforced them by lining four kitchen stools beneath the bottom bar?

We tried to shake his priorities back into place. We really did, ehn.

> "Do not hate me.
> The ears hear but the heart ignores it."

a wept "But when?" soon followed.

> "The time for crying has not yet come."

We blew rage through the lofty pawpaw leaves and cast one fruit to the ground, sent the seeds like fleeing ants from a flooded home creeping into the flesh between Msanide's toes.

but this time, when the earth's undulation tripped him over, he screamed, waking himself up.

> "Stupid boy."

his mother jolted awake. "Ni chani, Msanide?"

Msanide found the shadowy window, organza cascading from nails near the galvanized roof to the floor. the orange outline of the mosquito coil still puffing smoke into the bedroom. he wondered how recently he and Kachila had been pillowed on their mother's chest. a clock ticked on the wall. *I am safe here.* he exhaled, recalling himself fighting sleep against the tendrils of his mother's voice dancing with dust motes in the bedroom; all while, Kachila sounded the parts of a bedtime story, "Kalulu fell asleep on the trail."

Msanide's heart was still frantic, but he said, "Nothing," to his mother, laughing again as if Kachila was still squealing, "Wake up Kalulu, wake up!" before they chorused the ending—"Kalulu overslept, and Tortoise won the race."

he's that same breathless now, asking, "It was my laughter, wasn't it, Dr. Chali?"

Dr. Chali angles herself toward him and closes the compact distance between them. the crevice linking her breasts exposes itself, "Your laughter?"

I bet she sprays her perfume right in that depression where her neck ends.

"Focus, iwe!"

Msanide stares at her delicate silver necklace. it swings and lands in the shadows of her blouse, darkening her neck like a fresh love bite. Msanide licks his lips, and she shifts back, smooths her skirt, and clears her throat.

"Did my laughter kill them?"

that night, his mother had said, "ThenwhyareyouscreamingMsanide?" as she rubbed sleep from her eyes.

Dr. Chali's sentence mashes into one word too, like overcooked beans.

"YoutellmeMsanide."

"Ma's voice used to do the same thing yours is doing."

"Because you and Kachila and him died," he'd told his irate mother then.

she'd defrosted quick, like a frozen chicken placed in boiling water. "Him?" she said, pulling the light cord and flooding the room with white.

Senior's name had already started to coagulate in him, but Msanide managed to say "Senior," because this was important. it was his father, after all, who was stuck on the other side of the crackling phone cords at a payphone next to the post office collecting a master's degree from America, not Kachila or their mother, or Msanide.

in his mother's mouth, though, Senior's name spurred a laugh—this floating thing that emerged from her throat to hang around the kitchen on Saturday mornings. Senior would tiptoe behind her as she fried vitumbuwa, and in a pretend whisper, while he winked at the children, he'd say, "Hmmm. My butterfly. Breakfast smells nice, but nothing is as lovely as you."

"Youdreamtaboutyourfather?" the mother.

"Ah-ah, this word again?"

"Whatismyvoicedoing?" Dr. Chali.

in both iterations of Msanide, he blinks back—quiet.

"I'd love to hear more about your mother's voice. This is the first time you are telling me about her. What was she like?"

"Easy."

"Like rain, Ma was," he laughs. which is the only way to say he doesn't remember the whole of her, just portions—the big swooping curls in her hair after a relaxer, the way her ears seemed to block everything out when *Passions* was on, chipped red polish on her fingernails—like standing in the memory of a just-passed storm while drenched to the bone.

"Is something funny?" she asks, patting the *inappropriate laughter* she's just written.

"No, but my reason for escaping sleep that night wasn't new, after all. It's not like I'd carried over the bedtime story like luggage. There was no human-rabbit child belonging to Kalulu and his human wife, no three little pigs as women, or greedy Chisamu rotting at the bottom of the well with all the pumpkins he refused to share with his wife and children."

We nod.

on her notepad, Dr. Chali's fingers grow furious. she mouths, *Chisamu*, *Kalulu*, and *Greedy*, while *strange use of words* makes its way across her page.

We smile—the doctor's welling attention to everything We're saying.

"I mean," he says, "it's not like I'd slit my wrists again while helping Cinderella take the broken glass out of her soles when her shoes broke on our veranda. Nothing ate its way out of my mind that night."

to his mother, Msanide had whispered, "I'm scared for Senior, Ma," and watched her smile grow as she stretched out the word *okay* like a yawn. "But it was just a dream, Msanide. Go back to sleep."

We kissed our teeth.

she slid back under her blanket.

"But—"

"It's late, iwe, please. Just sleep."

"Stupid woman."

"Ma. I'm scared."

"If you are afraid, then you must pray."

"It was just a dream."

"What was the dream?" asks Dr. Chali, penning this as *delusional thoughts and hallucinations*.

Msanide had found the floor and recited the prayer he'd learned at Sunday School, ending it with, "God, please protect Ma,"

"Amen," his mother sleepily agreed.

"and Kachila."

in his sleep, Msanide's brother wheezed. he was dressed in sole-to-neck pajamas, yet still, the May air flooded his chest and frustrated his breathing. asthma, the hospital had named it at his birth.

"and Daddy."

Msanide held his breath.

when his mother summoned her God, her tears would stream; she'd convulse and retreat into a language Msanide couldn't untangle. she'd emerge from the experience with a soft hum on her lips for the rest of the day.

but Msanide's relief does not come.

his mother says, "Oh, baby, bwela che ugone, ehn?" and pats his spot on the mattress. "Daddy will be back soon. I promise."

a wisp of his father strolls through Arrivals.

but not before the university senate accuses him of deserting and throwing them and their furniture out of the university house, with its three bedrooms and cold floor tiles.

—not before their mother rents four rooms in Wusakile and calls it home,

—not before the guava tree grows out of its pruning and promises more seedy, sweet fruit,

—not before Kachila chips his front teeth in a tumble down the kitchen steps,

—not before the Ministry of Health delays the nurses' salaries by three months until their mother is forced to trade beef stews and spinach in peanut sauce for boiled eggs, then sautéed tomatoes, then finally, neat little piles of salt to dip their nsima into at supper.

Senior hadn't heard Kachila wail "I want Daddy!" because he wasn't full after one of those measly lunches, as though Senior would appear at the door with buttered sliced bread and Fanta.

he didn't see his wife squeeze Msanide's wrist after. or hear her hiss, "Don't say that, iwe," because Msanide told Kachila "Don't cry for Senior. He's dead to us!" snatching the wail out of the younger brother's mouth instantly.

but on those monthly phone calls before Senior's return, Kachila said "I love you" back into the receiver, ignoring Msanide's stare burning through his skull. so, no surprises when Kachila squeals "Daddy!" at the man smiling behind the trolley piled with suitcases the boys would dig through later.

Msanide stared up and measured the markers of his father.

—his afro was still there, with fresh scatterings of gray,

—he had swapped his round eyeglasses for a frame with a wire traveling from the arch of one eyebrow to the next,

—his skin, sun-starved now, was a quieter brown. when Senior finally said "It's so good to be home," he rushed over the consonants as though his tongue had lay dormant too long and, in the time elapsed, had forgotten itself,

—and when he looked down at Msanide, said "Junior, uli bwa?" Senior's greeting was like that of the visiting Muzungu teachers who emphasized the wrong part of a name.

but it had been 292 days without this endearment and something yielded in Msanide's gut. "Daddy?" he said, and flung himself around his father.

at home, their neighbors peeped over their clotheslines and watched the taxi park next to the veranda.

"Don't open any windows," instructio-warned Msanide's mother, "unless you want to invite witches inside to steal our blessings."

his parents locked themselves in the bedroom after telling Msanide to take Kachila outside to play if he tried to knock and disturb them. the sounds creeping out of the locked door—slapping interjected by their parents' grunts were swallowed by the boys' hands rummaging. hours wound past, with the brothers examining skinny perfume bottles, fat, bright storybooks, makeup palettes that Kachila would mistake for watercolors, shoes that lit up when they stomped, piles of chiffon dresses, and toy cars tiny enough to fit in the open boot of Msanide's wire cars.

that first week of Senior's return was almost like the hushed years before the airplane took him. but on this side of Senior's return, when Saturday morning came, Senior left before breakfast and demoted their mother's laugh to evening. Senior returned mumbling about failed government deals and "Fuck!" the "Senate."

the university had made him beg, then refused to reinstate him.

"Look at this man, making me worry for nothing," Msanide's mother snickered as Senior's rocking body approached.

she refused to open the door at first, instead shifting her shoulders up and down as she paced the corridor.

"Ignore him," she told the boys when Senior rapped against the bedroom window with "Junior, open for Senior."

but when he began pleading minutes later, she unlocked the door to call him an idiot as he stumbled in. in return, he shoved her shoulder. she stumbled back. "Sorry, sorry, my love," he said.

"You want to fight, ehn? Beat me, you half-man!"

when Senior complied, Msanide's mother grabbed her cheek and shrieked, "You slapped me? Msanide, you slapped me? You—"

all while Msanide whispered, "Stop. Please, stop," until Kachila started to bawl.

"Now look what you did," she scolded. "You've gone and scared the children."

but then, just when it seemed like Senior's eyebrows would never unravel again, like maybe he'd do something with the fist he'd balled by his trouser pocket, Senior leaned into her and smacked a loud kiss onto her mouth, pulling her laughter out of her in bright spurts.

"You're so silly," she said between giggles, propping him up. "You must be hungry, come."

arm in arm, they walked into the kitchen, where the aroma of hot nsima bubbling in a pot would soon follow.

but each Saturday after, Msanide could swear Senior returned a little more shrunken into himself, the *Fucks* just a little bit louder. so, though Senior's shirts still clung to his shoulders, and the rivers of veins in his neck still throbbed when he was annoyed. although he still bent at the kitchen door to avoid bumping his head against the frame, Msanide asked, "Senior, is it possible for adults to grow smaller?"

"Of course, it is. Just when they think they are done growing,"

Senior guffawed.

"their bodies start sliding backward in time."

"No, Junior, impossible," he assured Msanide.

so the thought, Msanide figured, of Senior gradually fading since his return must have been a phantom thing.

"The ears hear but the heart ignores it."

the Zambia Meteorological Department would call our ensuing laughter a tremor on the 19.00 hours news.

and this Msanide's mind was too congested with the excitement of Senior taking Kachila and him to the Trade Fair to notice. the brothers ate an entire box of EET SUM MORS on the bus ride out of Kitwe and Senior hadn't cared about all the crumbs they scattered on his lap as the brothers giggled at everything and nothing.

Ndola town was dusty, cold, and happy on the other side of the many ticket gates. somehow, the moos from the animal show, gun salutes, a lone train chugging through the grounds had managed to sit in the same space as all of the grown-up voices telling their children to stay close if they didn't want to get stolen.

the climax, a greasy chicken and chips lunch later, was Msanide licking green candy floss as a clown with a vulgar grin painted his arm gold and yellow in an overstretched H for He-man. all the while, Kachila's laughter swooped up and dipped with his merry-go-round ride.

"Do you know magic, doctor Chali?" Msanide asks

"No." she writes *disorganized thinking (speech),* but says, "What is magic?"

"My father flashing us his nicotine-stained smile with his arms folded over his shirt at the trade fair—*that* was magic?"

she writes *irrational statements,* nods and asks, "So, how did we get from there to here, Msanide?"

"I've already told the lawyer everything."

"There are still some blanks to fill in. Only you can tell me. Msanide, listen to me. The court would like to know, for example, what happened before the police arrived at your house? Did you and your Dad have a fight?"

Msanide shrugs.

flat, expressionless gaze, her pen says. to Msanide, "Then where is Kachila now?"

"Here!"

in a hole of flames. "Dead."

under her breath, "Okay, progress," then, "and how did he die?"

"The coughing. The coughing fits were too much for his body."

"Correct! Your brother had tuberculosis. Thanks for telling me the truth."

a doctor's word for Kachila's lungs refusing to listen to the pills and injections. For the blood-tinged sputum his body ejected, which made his mother say, "He's dying. My baby. God. My baby is dying," in a voice smaller than anything Msanide thought could exist.

Msanide closes his eyes and allows us to crawl into him, spread a carpet of goose pimples all over his arms.

"What happened next?" Dr. Chali asks.

his mother refused the help of her sisters at the service is what. she walked to the front of the church unaided and read from her bedside Bible. "I love the Lord, for he heard my voice; he heard my cry for mercy. Because he turned his ear to me, I will call on him as long as I live."

"The cords of death entangled me, the anguish of the grave came over me; I was overcome by distress and sorrow," Msanide says.

"Msanide, no." Dr. Chali snaps her fingers. "Try and remember. We're here to get to the bottom of the circumstances surrounding your father's death. Did he beat you first or something?"

"Then I called on the name of the Lord:"

she says, "I know you can understand me, Msanide." but writes, *unable to concentrate.* "I know you can understand me, Msanide. You've already said so much. You're doing really well. Stay with me. What made you hit him with that vase?"

"Lord, save me!"

but when Msanide's mother said "Amen," at the end of her reading, the tears didn't come, and she forgot her after-prayer hum.

Saturday mornings evolved into nights Senior returned with eyes stained the color of dry blood. the trick he played failed to pull her laugh out. when she opened the door, his fist took turns painting her face a moonless sky black.

"Stop. Please, stop," Msanide says.

the doctor replies, "Okayokayletstalkaboutyourfatherinstead."

"What the eye sees, the heart should not forget."

between his mother following Kachila and Senior drowning in his gin, Msanide forgot our "Calamity does not warn" and our echo of 8th November. he counted himself lucky when Senior told him to throw away all his empty bottles, promised, "We'll start again, Junior mwandi." a tight little lie, told and retold month after month in different houses before landladies demanded their dues until finally, both men hear the crash against the elder one's head, see red before one body slackens and falls.

"Msanide, talk to me."

Senior's death certificate will say 2008, yes, but his coming undone began the moment Kachila's coughing ceased. by the time mother followed son four months later, Senior was like a jersey caught in a door hinge left to unravel. his wife had been the needle, both children his wool. who would stitch him back now?

"Do not hate me." once.

"Msanide," Dr. Chali repeats.

"Do not hate me." twice.

Msanide's eyes roll in to meet us.

"Do not hate me."

Msanide's reply is a gaunt, drawled out, "Ma?" that springs Dr. Chali from her seat. she abandons the folder and pen and undecided hand-writing. she rushes to the door, fights lock with key and mouths "God," and "Msanide," and "what is this?" and "open, open, open," until the door complies.

but he hears us.

"Finally."

the door swings open, meows rush in, and Dr. Chali shouts, "I need help with this patient!"

Msanide says, "Calamity does not warn. But what enters the ear stays for good. On your unlucky day, even cold food will burn you. This is how the tree falls to the ground, but the earth feels its pain."

"Yes," We laugh.

HAIL MARY

I'm crammed in with forty-nine other pairs of feet, shackled in steel. It's kinda like a reverse Oreo of Forest Park, Detroit, you know? All fire-white walls, ceilings, and floors, brimming with chocolate faces, nothing like home.

We're all waiting on the judge to waltz in and decide from the looks of us if we're worth the shiny card. In my mind, I'm scrambling at a prayer, trying to grasp at words I haven't recited for twenty, maybe thirty years, but time has erased what was once glued to my mind like peanut butter to bread. Now I have to pry the words out, calm my racing heart, press my droopy lids together before I can pray, *Hail, Mary, full of grace.*

I stare down at the gap between my boobs where a blue rosary has hung since '88, and beg the beads to guide the angelic salutation back to me. It's flaky and faded, but a prayer is a prayer, right? God is God? I wait for the words to come. *Nothing.*

The AC is blasting winter in the middle of spring, but from the wet patches on our orange jumpsuits and the stench of sweat, it's kinda like July in here instead of mid-March.

The clock says it's a quarter to nine, fifteen minutes to go. There are four cops poised up front, three disguised in gray suits and one in a black T-shirt instead of the navy and white.

I dig for the prayer again, recalling my mother's husky voice the last time she saw me, reminding me as always to pray: "Kopaila." And for a moment, I'm just a kid again, kneeling on the rough floor of our room in Kanyama Compound, saying the Hail Mary. But when I open my eyes, I'm still stuck here, next to the bright flag of a country I've been trying to claim as my own since I first abandoned mine.

There are other times I have tried to pray.

October 1996, squeezing my eyes in St. Joseph's, trying to breathe when the midwife says to, in between the pain splitting me open, praying I would live through it. That the babies would be healthy. That I wouldn't be in there too long. The bill not too crippling. The state insurance should cover it.

Boxing Day 2015, outside the coat factory in Harper Woods, when I found myself in a crossfire between rival gangs. I prayed to live. Swore to go to confession the next day. Prayed to get out before the cops arrived and started hauling every Black body they saw into their wailing cars.

Twenty-seven years old, sitting at a crammed dinner table, staring at a turkey the size of two men's heads stammering as Jamie's mom asked, "Aren't you too young for marriage, baby?" Whole time she was cradling Jamie's head, rubbing the bald spot growing in the middle and staring at me like we was on a playground fighting for the attention of a boy. For the longest moment I didn't answer, thinking how I wasn't sure if she was asking me or she was asking her son. But before I could get my words formed nice, Jamie said, "Nah, Ma, she takes care of me good. Try her potato salad." I prayed that the woman across from me wouldn't see through me. Prayed that she would ignore the sweat in my pits, which I felt sure she could smell. And I prayed that the wedding would come soon so we could get the paperwork started.

The last one helps me find my gap-toothed smile, one I thought I had lost somewhere in the two-something years I've been caged. It plants a hope that, maybe, Jamie and the girls are waiting on the other side of the wooden doors to go home with me and forget the last two years ever happened. Jamie's "Marry me, baby," the look in his eyes was like maybe he'd been waiting all his life to kneel down and look up at me.

So that "Yes!" I kinda meant it.

I prayed the marriage would make the stamp easier.

But then came babies, and rent, and after-school activities, and, and, and—nothing left for immigration lawyers good enough to fix my mess.

"What are you smiling for?" barks a man. He is all muscle and gleaming black skin, stunning if I met him anywhere but here. I raise my head to glare at him, a curse kissing my lips with the tip of my tongue, but words will only land me in more trouble, so I bow my head and keep my trap closed.

He smirks like he knows, brushes his smooth fingers over the gun on his hip, and puffs up, stretching the words etched in white on his black T-shirt: POLICE ICE.

The Lord is with thee.

For six hundred and seventy-seven days, I've grumbled about the snail-like pace of the proceedings. For twenty-two months, I sneered inwardly each time I was told to repeat my particulars, *for the record*: "Chibotu Mainga. Zambian. Born February 17, 1964."

But now that the day is finally here, all my groanings have dissolved into silence, my own thoughts, a muddled mixture of the half-truths and lies I'll tell—my life in five minutes or less.

I have a husband and two children who depend on me emotionally.

I fear prosecution in my home country.

I volunteer at the animal rescue shelter.

The United States has been my home for over thirty years.

In Zambia, I'll face discrimination due to my tribal background.

Until my arrest for skipping a red light two years ago, I had lived a life free of crime.

Paid my bills.

Eight fifty. On any other Friday, I would be cleaning messes at the home on Woodward Avenue, dragging on a Slims when my supervisor wasn't looking. Now it's all I can do not to reach up and force the hands of the clock to still.

I scan the faces around me, as solemn as mourners in a graveyard.

Across from me is the scrunched-up face of a cocoa-skinned woman, coughing and wringing her wrinkled hands, her mane of curls damp with sweat.

Behind her, a man is muttering to himself, bobbing his head back and forth toward his stubby fingers pressed together in prayer. His face is crumpled and red.

To his left is a gaunt man, sweat dripping into his open palms; he catches me looking at him, and I cast my eyes downward, suddenly aware of my body, vibrating to the rhythm of my heart.

Eight fifty-five. A door opens, letting another guard in. He carries with him the rich aroma of freshly ground coffee, jarring me with the memory of walking past the carousels of Hartsfield–Jackson Atlanta International Airport back in April of '88. With that, I picture the other things I've learned to love: the colors of fall—the leaves transforming from lush green to burnt orange, peppering the tarred roads golden; a deceptive sun that glowed over the streets in winter and chilled the bones instead of warmed.

Eight fifty-seven.

I crave to finger the cross on my rosary.

"Look up!" spits the ICE man.

"Yes, sir," I say, folding my knuckles into fists.

Blessed art thou amongst women, and blessed is the fruit of thy womb, Jesus.

It's nine o'clock when the judge walks in; even the chains around our ankles shut up. The courtroom is a vacuum to the humming sounds of Michigan, which seep in through a lone window on my left.

An ambulance wailing in the distance.

A dog barking.

The bass from a car stereo.

A police siren.

A gunshot.

The *ping* of train doors closing.

Tires screeching to a halt.

A screaming child.

Holy Mary, mother of God.

She sits and nods at us to do the same. We know the drill.

The first to be called is a babe in the back row. She shuffles to the podium to make her case.

"Raise your right hand," says one of the suited men.

"Levante a sua mão direita," follows the interpreter in Portuguese.

So, my language class at Macomb wasn't for nothing after all.

From her thin lips emerges a whimper—begging, grinding English and Portuguese into one mushed-up plea. She appears to have aged in the wait. As though her terror is streaking her auburn hair silver where the white light of the room hits it.

"Por favor," she says, kneeling, raising both hands. *Please.* Almost inaudibly as she moves farther from the microphone.

"Raise your right hand!"

She does so as she stands, without waiting for the interpretation.

Her rap is read out to her, translated, and then, after a forever of Portuguese words racing the English ones, at nine forty-five, the judge speaks: "On your own admission, you entered this country illegally and had sought to normalize your status. Your child is an American citizen, but you aren't, and you cannot ride on the tails of her legality to legitimize your stay." The judge looks up, something flashing across her eyes—pity, I decide.

"Meu Deus!" wails the woman, collapsing into sobs as she plods out of the courtroom, making all my fears real with each step. *My God!*

Panic shoots through me, paralyzing everything but my thoughts.

I'll miss my daughters' college graduations.

I won't see them get married.

Jamie won't follow me.

He won't survive a day there.

I can't—The next person rises from amid the crowd and swaggers to the podium, a gold tooth shining in his mouth. His jumpsuit is too large on his frame, and his right arm won't stop shaking, despite his defiant gait. He stares down the judge, refusing to bend, even as she reads the verdict: "Deportation ordered."

I guess it's really going down.

Ten o'clock.

A girl rises and glides to the front, kinda like she's in a ball gown and not jail gear.

No. She shakes her head. *She doesn't need an interpreter. Yes, she understands what that means.*

"Very well." The judge nods, turning to the pages on her desk.

The woman scopes the judge for a moment, her eyes glistening, ready to cry, but when she parts her lips to speak, she says, "It's okay, let me go!"

A murmur cuts through the hushed courtroom and stirs in me a brittle envy that tears at my throat. I watch in shock as she is led out of the room, gliding on those invisible stilettos, and I wish I could demand the same thing. But the wish dies before it can land on my tongue.

Pray for us sinners.

Eleven o'clock.

The next woman to go up front could be my sister but for the shock of blond hair framing her face. Even her walk, slow but steady, reminds me of my own before the chains. Her accent, saying *s* as a *z*, shifts me back home before this shitty dream began.

And when I squeeze my eyes shut, *I'm ten again, racing wire cars along a dusty street, against gusts of wind; then I'm twelve, in my mother's kitchen, inhaling the sweet aroma of boiled fresh maize; the next I'm in a slippery guava tree, biting into the near-rotting white-fleshed fruit in March. I'm in Kanyama Market, selling roasted groundnuts after school* with my brother; and then I'm a pimply teenager, standing at the unnamed street corner all day; and then I'm back here, staring at the blond shrugging off the ICE man when he tries to lead her out.

Twelve o'clock.

"Chibotu Mainga," says the judge, the middle syllable all warped in her mouth, *bow* instead of *bo* in my first name, the way all other Americans have done since I came here. I stand anyway and lumber to the podium.

Now and at the hour of our death.

I bore through my white sneakers, clench and unclench my toes in a dance with my fingers. Bracing myself for the fifteen-hour flight back to Zambia.

Who'll meet me?

What will my siblings think?

How would I explain my silence?

Why the Skype calls had stopped?

Why they no longer received a hundred dollars through Western Union on the fifteenth of the month?

And will they understand me, now that I swallow the d's and t's in my words and say each sentence like it's a question?

"Raise your right hand!"

I do, then ramble out the words I've waited twenty-two months to say: "My name is *Chibotu* Mainga.

"I moved to the United States when I was twenty-four, in April 1988, on a visitor's visa."

The judge is scribbling furiously—the verdict probably, not my words, but I continue anyway.

"I didn't leave, because my uncle fell ill and needed my care." I look up to make eye contact through my lie; she doesn't look back. "Since then, I've married and have twin daughters who're now twenty-two and studying at Wayne State University. I'm—I was a direct care worker—"

"I've heard the facts," she interjects, and a buzzing starts in my head. Her lips move, but I hear nothing until "You've satisfied the requirements to be permitted to stay in the United States of America."

"Say what?" A whisper, if that.

Amen.

"What?!" A shout, more than.

"We're adjourned for lunch," announces the judge.

The ICE man glowers at the judge and then at me before he stomps to free me.

I turn to face the exit, letting relief run in tears across my face. Then with each step, the full prayer swims back to mind, spilling out as sobs. "Hail, Mary, full of grace, the Lord is with thee. Blessed art thou amongst women, and blessed is the fruit of thy womb, Jesus. Holy Mary, mother of God, pray for us sinners now and at the hour of our death. Amen."

I shiver when I step outside; Jamie isn't there. Still, I smile, a real one this time, never happier to feel that lying white sun in the middle of a blue sky, chilling instead of warming the bones.

MASTITIS

Mwana ni mkhuzi wa ntegwa.
A child is the girdle of marriage.
—**Tumbuka proverb**

If I die right now, my husband will discover my body tomorrow morning propped up by two pillows, the silk of my nightdress glued to my skin with sweat. Every morning, Daliso tiptoes from the spare bedroom back into ours. He takes his three-minute shower, puts on a slim-fit suit and matching tie, and creeps out of the room in silence as if he's leaving a mistress instead of a wife he's only had for a year. We reconvene in public spaces—over the kitchen table, in front of the television, or separated by the center console in our shared red Fit.

If I am dead when he creeps back in tomorrow, will he notice?

Will it shock him to find my eyes agape as they've been all night? With the room etched perfectly in my pupils like chalk on a blackboard? Will he stop in the middle of patting his hair down and peer through the tiny eyes of the mosquito net hanging over Baby and me? Or will he shuffle on the other side of the mesh, past the mound of our dirty clothes peeking out of the washing basket to the wardrobe, and dust a jacket from the hanger like usual?

Will he just leave us here?

The blue light of my phone flashes. A reminder of the unread messages sitting in my WhatsApp inbox. The "My condolences on the death of your mother ☹" texts blinking with the "Congrats on the baby, please send pictures!" ones.

My head is a heavy bag of sand crushing my neck, unappeased even by the empty bottle of Tramadol accusing me on the bedside table.

But: I am not dead.

It's been a week since my mother passed. Since her sisters trickled down my parents' yard, dropped their handbags onto the half-moon welcome rug on the veranda, flung themselves to the floor, and wailed "Sanko!" into the tiles. As though out of the glazed ceramic Amama would answer them: "Ma!"

Seven black squares in December to mark the amount of time elapsed since Baby was born and plunged me into motherhood. Seven long days since a match lit in my gut and started searing through me from the inside out.

The old wooden clock in the sitting room announces 2:00 a.m. with two teeth-grinding chimes, as though I need any more reminders of my wakefulness.

But sleep is worse.

The night before Amama's burial I tried, foolishly, to plan my dream, hoping I could trick sleep into being bearable again by replaying my last private conversation with her—the one when she'd promised me that children drew husbands closer to their wives even in the worst marriages. Amama had said this with the certainty of someone who'd lived it.

"Truth-God!"

She'd even sworn it, flicking one forefinger toward heaven. As though that was why they'd only had me. Not, like the family gossip went, because Amama got married too late—thirty-five, took another five years to conceive me, and then her womb dried up. Not because my father was already fifty-three by then, widowed, childless, and on his second wife. And yet, I had believed her.

Truth-God.

In slumber that night, a nightmare clawed at me instead of Amama's balming words. Her limbless head bobbed in a black vacuum, scolding me:

 —Ah-ah, iwe, feed your child.

 —Take a shower; you are starting to smell.

 —Get out of that nightdress and put on some proper clothes.

 —Comb that hair. You'll scare away your poor husband.

 —Truth-God, Zaliwe, husbands don't like dirty wives.

 —He'll leave you.

I could have told her: Daliso doesn't care if I am draped in a sweat-stained nightie or squeezed into a bandage dress and heels. Fikuti or flowing Brazilian weave—it doesn't matter to him.

Instead, I'd bitten down my responses, glad to see my mother again, even if only her face was alive, even if it was just a dream.

The next morning, when I awoke with a bloodied lip from where my teeth had sunk into my skin, I was grateful the ache in my chest had migrated to the swollen cut.

Now I run my tongue over the lip, no longer puffed up, and sigh.

God. In my arms, Baby continues to fuss despite my endless rocking. She rubs her tiny fists against her lips, twisting herself in the fleece of her romper, kicking against the jagged wound across my abdomen.

I try again to quiet her: "Shhh." I slip the strap of my nightdress down my shoulder and bring Baby's face to my breast. She finds the tip of my nipple with her mouth. Her eyelids flutter as she unclenches her tiny palms and her little body relaxes. My nipple burns when she suckles, then tightens when she releases it. Slowly, her mouth forms a tiny upside-down U, which wrinkles her chin as if I am draining bile into her.

I shift my weight on the mattress, move Baby away from my scar, and groan. "What do you want from me?"

Every morning I bathe this child in a basin of lukewarm water. I seal the moisture in with Vaseline and pat her down with Johnson's powder. I swaddle her in blankets and rock her until we both grow weary. But I know if she could answer me, Baby would probably say, *Milk.*

The one thing I cannot give her.

The nurse had assured me when she discharged us: "The more you feed her, the faster the milk will come." Google tells me not to worry because "it can take up to four days for milk to come in for first-time mums." Even my mother-in-law, petite as she is, front as flat as her back, had wisdom to share. "Two weeks," she exclaimed, illustrating the length of time by wagging two fingers in my face. "I had no milk for two long weeks—now look at Daliso." She beamed up at her eldest son, "He grew up to be a giant!"

My breasts have disregarded it all—the nurse's smiling promises, Google search results, Daliso's proud mother. They are just two swollen glands weighing my chest down. Balls have formed inside them. The tension has spread into my neck and shoulders, throbbing in unison with my pulse.

I let my eyes close and watch stars dart across the inside of my eyelids. I hold my breath. For one-tenth of a minute, it's only mosquitoes buzzing around us, crickets singing outside, rumbling music in the distance and on the other side of the bedroom wall, Daliso's uneven snoring—the newest soundtrack to our marriage. When I exhale, Baby wails.

Yes, if I died right now, Daliso would find my arms still a pendulum.

I glare down at the child—the one who killed my mother merely by being born. Although when the memory comes into view, as it does now, I cannot tell which came first.

Was it my mother falling, or the belt of pain tightening around my abdomen until Baby was pulled out of me?

Amama and I had been shopping for chitenges in Safique's. One moment we were picking out the fabric from the wall of hanging cloth for post-delivery outfits, because, as Amama kept reminding me, "You must still look beautiful for your husband even after you have your children," and the next she was splayed across the linoleum floor, clutching the left side of her chest. Then everything turned black.

When I came to, I was looking at a water splotch fanning out from muddy brown to the white of the rest of the ceiling. My torso was covered in a faded blue hospital gown and a pile of blankets, but I was shivering. I pinched my nose against the sting of disinfectant, methylated spirits, and blood. My mind spooled backward—my body on a stretcher, being lifted into a van, a distant voice asking me to say my name, someone holding me up, a needle cold against my back, tin-gling, numbness from the waist down, a baby, wrinkled, bloodied, and screaming.

A nurse came into view, white cap first, starched uniform next, then the yellow bundle in her arms.

I shook my head at her slowly, my gaze falling on the cannula sticking out of my left hand. I was still two weeks from my due date.

"Where's my mother?" I demanded.

Instead of telling me, the stupid woman smiled, tucked her head into her neck, and said, "Both you and the baby were under a lot of distress. But we thank God, the doctors were able to deliver your baby safely. It's a girl."

She made as if to place the bundle on my chest. I recoiled, scrambled around the bedding, frantic until I found my stomach. My heart began to pound. I held the deflated flab of skin and felt the stretch marks crawling in every direction until my fingers met a tender spot beneath my navel and a crooked line of raised stitches that I didn't have before.

I cut the nurse a look. "That"—I jabbed the air between us—"is not mine."

She clicked her tongue. "This is your first time, ehn? Don't worry. You'll have a boy next time."

I kissed my teeth. What a complete idiot! Amama had held my hand at the twenty-week appointment. And when the sonographer had said "Congratulations, it's a boy!" Amama had clapped and said "Boy or girl, a child is a blessing," dropping her voice on the third word as though if she said it too loudly the technician might change his mind and say *girl* rather than *boy*.

I had even said "Amen," sealing it in with a prayer.

That grainy image that had flickered on the little screen in that office was my child. My son was due on the first of January 2018, not what this nurse was trying to pass off.

"Where's my phone?" I snapped. "What's the date?" My voice was shaking.

"Nineteenth of December," she said softly, handing me the phone.

Something calcified in my throat like a half-chewed, raw sweet potato. The acrid taste racing across my tongue.

An entire day?

"Where is my mother?"

This time, the question crawled out, unsure if it wanted to be asked.

The nurse glanced down as though the answer was buried in the blanket. When she looked back at me, her eyes had glossed over. Gently, she placed the bundle on my chest and slowly backed out of the room.

I steadied my fingers over the keypad on my phone and dialed my mother's number.

An automated voice answered: "The mobile subscriber you have dialed is either outside the coverage area or has their phone switched off. Please try your call later."

"Have you eaten?" I texted Amama anyway. Because why else would she have fainted? Safique's wasn't even that packed when we were there—it was only nine in the morning.

When my phone buzzed, the message I clicked open was from a cousin whom I'd last seen at my wedding.

"My condolences, cuz. MHSRIP."

I slumped back and lay there, motionless until my husband arrived.

Daliso clasped my palm in his and said, "Babes." Five little letters, strung together to liquefy my insides. He hadn't called me that since I told him I was pregnant. I remember thinking for a fleeting moment how I'd tell Amama she was right. That babies could spin resentment back into love.

"Yes, babes?" I whispered back.

He fiddled with my fingers, pursed his lips, and then said. "Mum passed away." He didn't say *your mum*, so I wrapped my fingers around his and hoped.

I watched his lips move until I caught the sympathy in his eyes when he told me that my mum had a stroke. "There was nothing more they could do," he said, wearing the pity-you expression of an American sitcom doctor. "I'm so sorry."

They could have saved her!

He didn't resist when I shook him off.

My mother? Who walked to and from Kamwala Market every day just for the exercise? The same mother who had replaced sunflower oil with olive and refined breakfast mealie meal with roller meal?

"No," I corrected him. *Not Amama.*

"Sorry," he muttered.

Daliso averted his eyes and lifted Baby from my chest. He rocked her awhile, glancing beyond her head, into the purple cloud of jacarandas hanging outside the hospital window. He mumbled something about needing to assist with Amama's funeral arrangements, get our house ready for Baby, and call off work. Gingerly, he placed Baby back in my arms and walked out of the room.

Right then, as loudly as if he'd said the words, a thought planted itself in my mind, as crisp as the soles of Daliso's shoes clicking away: it's not that he doesn't want a girl, it's that he doesn't want a child—not this one, or any other. Why else would he suddenly be behaving this way? Clenching when I rub my hand down his arm or slip my tongue between his lips when I kiss him?

I shivered.

It was either that or . . . ?

I wrapped my arms around myself, warding off the unfinished thought.

From the spare bedroom, Daliso punches our shared wall. "For fuck's sake, Zaliwe!"

"What?"

"Some of us have work in the morning. Shut that baby up!"

It's the most we've said to each other since Amama passed. He says it like he is the only person employed. As if, before Baby, we didn't ride our little red Fit into town every morning. Like I didn't have a half-circular office at the Cairo Road branch of Zanaco, where I sat on most days sealed off from the long queues of customers behind glass and air conditioning. Like I didn't have a golden placard that said *Manager* glued to my door. Like he is the only one who supervises a team of five, whose office orderly curtsies when he walks into a room. Before Baby, we used to be friends: Daliso and me. We'd get drunk together, stagger out of Chicago's giggling at nothing. We'd leave our car in the parking lot and overpay a taxi driver to take us back home. I should have known from the way he'd collapse into bed with me, both with our sweaty clothes still on, and fall asleep without even trying to have sex with me.

Foolish me.

I'd assumed when Daliso bent me over and slipped into me once a month he accepted that what followed marriage would be children. I'd been arrogant enough not to believe that I was more than a veil for what he really wanted. Never seen myself as just the convenient best friend he married to silence his mother's "When will you marry?"

"Want to trade places?" I shoot back at him through gritted teeth.

When he doesn't answer, I want to jump out of the sheets and slap him. But jumping requires strength and my eyes are starting to sting, blurring the room into a rain-gray cloud. I imagine Daliso sprawled across the bed we'd been preparing for Amama to sleep in while she helped me with our child when the time came. In my mind's eye, I see his feet hanging over the edge, his mouth slightly open, drool collecting in his stubble. My hand reaches for Daliso's side of the bed, tracing the slight impression of his head in the pillow. If not for the weight in my arms, I'd lean into it just for the faint notes of citrus from his shampoo, which I know still linger there.

If not for the weight in my arms, Daliso would be asleep there, sleep-talking in chopped-up sentences.

"—I love—"

"—our secret—"

"—okay?"

The afternoon when I called my husband from the bathroom stall at work, with my underwear still hanging around my ankles, and whispered "I'm pregnant" breathlessly, something shifted between us.

"Oh? That's good." His muted reply conveyed that it was everything but.

A boy, Amama had sworn, would snap him out of whatever nonsense was making him distant. "Every man wants a junior."

Are you sure? I want to ask Amama now. Instead, I croak the first half of my mother's name, "Ama—" and the rest of it dies in my throat. She would know what to do.

The little green tent that had been pitched in between my mother's petunias and the sprawling mulberry tree to mark her death has now been folded and packed away. The fire that told neighbors there was a funeral is now ash, swept away with the dirt. The fight between my father and my mother's family about the burial site is over. A priest stood over the open grave, prayed for her eternal rest while she was lowered into the ground in a coffin the same brown as her skin, glowing the way she would when she slathered herself with glycerine. The mourners have all returned to their lives. They've probably buried their black vitambalas under prettier headscarves. I must now gather what is left of me, rummage a smile for people when they ask how I am doing, and nod. "Nili bwino."

The funeral rites are over. My grief must trail behind it, like the convoy of cars that tailed each other from Kamwala to Memorial Park Cemetery. It must sink itself into the damp earth along with Amama's gleaming coffin.

Baby howls again.

Her father fists the wall, demanding silence. I bring Baby to the pit between my breasts, stifle her voice with my chest, and pull off the net. "Shhh," I say, slipping into my pata-patas. We tiptoe past Daliso's closed door. I push the living room door open with my back, Baby wriggling in my hands.

This part of the house gets more sound from outside. No one has told our neighbors that it's 2:00 a.m. or that my husband, who has work in the morning, needs sleep. Fireworks are shooting into the night, the Black Eyed Peas blasting out of their speakers.

Christmases past, Daliso and I would be hosting the neighborhood Christmas party. Me, smiling under the haze of too many bottles of Savanna, waving Daliso off as he whispered something into my ear. Him, walking into the house with his lifelong best friend, Matthew.

Tonight, I catch the sound of tires humming over the tarmac. Conductors are yelling "Mukwela" as minibuses make their rounds through Shantumbu Road for whoever is crazy enough to be walking in Chalala at this hour. I flip the light switch and squint.

Stiffly, I walk over to the window.

What would happen, I ask myself, *if I just laid her between the throw pillows on the sofa, took the keys dangling on a nail next to the door, and left her there? If I unlocked the gate and answered one of the Mukwelas on the other side of the fence, boarded a bus, and allowed myself to be swallowed by the metal jalopy into the blinking lights of Lusaka? Would Daliso finally bring himself to look at Baby's face long enough to find his reflection in it: sparse brows, high cheeks, and loopy right eye? Would he text Matthew and tell him I'd finally gone and invite him over to take my place on the left side of our bed? Or would he give our landlord a month's notice on our lease and move into Matthew's high-rise apartment in Kabulonga?*

Last month I stalked Daliso there in a blue taxi with windows tinted so dark I had to lean against the black film to see through it. At the end of the paved driveway was our red Fit, glimmering like an invitation for me to enter. I steeled myself to storm in and scream my husband's name until he emerged from one of the four flats. I'd been ready to tell

Matthew to stay away from my husband. But when the taxi driver, drumming his fingers on the steering wheel, asked me "Tingene?"

I shook my head, feeling suddenly stupid.

What kind of a wife lost her husband to another man?

Daliso thinks me too foolish to know the real reason he moved out of our room. Matthew's name flashes on his phone screen more often than his own mother's. Nothing to be suspicious of. Matthew is one of the boys. A brother. Best friends since they met in grade eight at Kafue Boys' Secondary School. They owned matching red Liverpool FC shirts and ate their pregame nsima at my table before heading to watch the matches at a bar. Matthew had helped Daliso pick my ruby engagement ring. He'd choreographed the bridal party's entrance for our wedding. He'd brought a breast pump to my baby shower, wrapped in an electric-blue fabric folded to mimic a diaper.

Now Matthew kept my husband on the phone until Daliso's battery threatened to die and then some more while it was connected to the charger on one end and Daliso's ear on the other.

Last Christmas, he and Daliso had emerged from the house, faces gleaming with sweat, hastily tucking shirts into their trousers before they strolled back to the smoking braai to stand with the other men.

"Babies," Amama had assured me as my pregnancy progressed, "only take long when they are in the womb." Through the nausea, the spitting, and my insatiable craving for roadside roasted cassava, Amama told me, "Once he is born, you'll see. Children grow as fast as you blink."

I blink down at Baby. "Shhh." I rock her past the black television, into the dining room, and then the kitchen.

The floor feels unsteady and the stench of meat gone bad expands in the air around us.

Fucking ZESCO! Electricity—but no, we haven't had a power outage in days.

I rush to open the fridge anyway, expecting slick fruit and graying meat, already counting how much rot this power cut will cost us, but the light flicks on as always, and for a breath, I just stand there, stunned.

Something shuffles in the corner. My body stiffens. My head turns slowly. My straw broom and a long mop are bundled together.

Shit, I hope we don't have mice.

The swift memory of the time we had them at my parents' house is enough to sheathe the skin on my arms in a carpet of goose pimples. Ndiyo, Amama called them, even after the Rattex, with which my father laced the molding of the house, killed them. The smell of their tiny decomposing bodies stank for weeks until we discovered them behind the sack of mealie meal. There was a big one and a barely formed one. Mother and child, I'd imagined, which my mother was calling "relish" and insisting that the reason she never got sick was that she was raised on a steady diet of roasted mice and nsima.

My stomach churns. No! If I have mice, I'll have to catch them another way. I raise my leg and kick one slipper into my palm, then I inch toward the movement, listening for the squeaking of mice. Instead, the broom shimmies out of the shadows into the light, past the table and chairs, toward me.

The slipper drops from my hand. I gasp, squeeze my eyelids together, and shake the image out of my head. But when I open my eyes, it's still there—the thin handle wrapped in strips of rubber, like line after tight line of black necklaces, wound around a narrow brown neck. Its thatched-grass body is bent to one side, like a cocked head. I blink, but no hand materializes to keep the object in place.

"Nilota," I say as I carefully reach for Baby's head. Her fontanelle pulses under my fingers. With my free hand, I feel my scalp between my unraveling cornrows and, although I feel my skin, hot under my fingers, I repeat myself: "I'm dreaming."

Amama's favorite disciplinary item, which she yielded whenever I talked back as a child, sweeps closer and stops just short of my feet.

"You are not dreaming, Zaliwe," says the mop, shimmying out into the light.

The voice is still my mother's. Climbing an octave on the third syllable of my name like she'd spent her whole day laughing and didn't have anything left in her chords to finish the word. Amama could fill up a room with her laughing voice alone. Where mine was kapenta in a bowl of water, hers was tilapia, large and filling. You couldn't look away from her if you wanted.

If she were standing where the mop now is, her hands would stretch out in front of her. Amama would take Baby from me and sing "Auwe" until Baby slept. If this were my mother, my heart would thump steadily, my hands would be calm, and my mind would be quiet, not racing in circles inside my head.

The sound of Amama's laughter spills out of the walls, dances in the air, and shoots through me.

No.

I take a giant step over to the sink. I pull out a baby bottle from the stack where a box of them sit, unused.

No.

I open the tap, fill the bottle halfway and then move it. I run my hand under the tap.

No.

The water turns hot when I swivel the knob toward the red. "Ouch!" I yelp.

"I'm here," the stove says.

"But—"

Amama's voice severs what's left of my doubt. "But what?" There is a lightness to her tone.

She knows all my *buts*. From the trivial "But I was still playing," "But I put enough water in the pot of beans—I did not expect them to burn," to the grave "But he is cheating, Amama, I know it! I wash his underwear, cook all his food, and give him my body, but he just doesn't want any of it."

Baby whimpers.

I place the teat on her mouth.

"No!"

The ceiling is talking.

The broom rises and smacks my feet, the way Amama would if I entered the house without slipping off my school shoes first. "What do you think you're doing?"

"I forgot to take my shoes off?" I say from memory.

Cutlery clinks in a drawer somewhere and takes the shape of Amama's chuckle. "I mean"—her voice grows tender—"I mean, what are you trying to feed my grandchild?" I purse my lips. "She's too young to drink water, you know."

I know. I've read all the "Breast Is Best" articles and attended all my antenatal classes. "But…" My voice hitches nonetheless.

"But chani?"

Me or her asking this one?

All she seems to do is fidget in her short bouts of sleep and wake up to cry is what I want to say. "I'm so tired" is what I do say.

Her voice liquefies. "Babies cry, Zaliwe. That's just how they talk."

"Truth-God?" I roll my eyes and place the teat against Baby's mouth again.

This time the broom smacks both of my feet. "Ah-ah!" Amama exclaims. The sound of teeth being sucked follows. "Not that, iwe!"

Now, this is the Amama of my childhood, who would stop her sweeping of the yard if she caught me crawling up a mango tree and toss the broom at my legs to force me back down. I scratch the spot the broom grazed—*Na funta*. I nod. Because why else would I be imagining this if not madness. A laugh rises in my throat, but when it comes out, I am crying.

"It's okay," she says. "I just want to help you, enh?"

I feel for a counter and put the bottle there. The broom and mop swivel to face it.

I say, "By starving her?"

"A child will eat what the mother eats." She used to use this phrase on me when money didn't stretch as long as the days of the month. Those months when she'd tell me to run over to a neighbor's house to say: "Amama sent me to ask for a tomato from you; she will give you back next week." Or holding a teacup: "Lend us tu salt tungono."

"How?" One word, but somehow splintered.

Baby's cry is growing, but Amama insists, "The milk will come."

"How, Amama?"

"Remind your body that your child is waiting to be fed." This tone was one Amama fell on when she had used up all her hardness but my stubbornness still refused to obey.

I square my shoulders and glance around the room. "Truth-God?"

"Truth-God," she whispers.

I can almost see her pointing to the skies, promising me this final truth.

I reach into my dress. Slowly, I bring my breast out and push my nipple into Baby's mouth, centimeter by painful centimeter, until all the black disappears between the pink of her lips.

"Hold it there."

I do.

"Keep your fingers on the bottom." The soft tone again. "And help her keep it in her mouth."

Baby latches onto the nipple, shooting fire up my breasts. The pain rides into my abdomen, forming a fist around my stomach, exactly like those first aches that delivered Baby to me. I wince.

"Awe! Do not take it out."

I narrow my eyes, reminding myself that it is me, Zaliwe Mwanza, Mulungushi University graduate. If I crane my neck, I can see the gold edges of the frame of my Best Graduating Student certificate in the living room. I cannot be talking to a broom. I shift my feet. Baby makes a sound, an almost gurgle that mellows the pain in my gut. I ease into it, pad slowly to the kitchen chairs across the room, and lower myself into a seat.

A release, like finally finding a toilet after being pressed for hours, washes over me.

I sigh, let my eyes close and stay that way until a chime from the clock startles me. As I rub the sleep out of my eyes, another chime rings out, and then a third. In the corner of the kitchen, the broom is tucked in place, unmoving. Baby's face is still glued to my chest, white pooling in the corners of her mouth. My free breast has leaked through my dress and onto my lap.

CHESS PIE

Imiti ikula é mpanga.
Growing trees are tomorrow's forests.

—Bemba proverb

The first time my mind scoops up Mom's words, packing them into me, all tight and tidy, I am five years old.

Mom's bent over the edge of the bathtub, cupping warm water with her hand and pouring it slow, all over my back, humming something I don't know. The skin around Mom's right eye is the color of her favorite cast iron, the shape of it like a knuckle. Her other eye is staring into a faraway place. It's as if she isn't really looking at me or the ducks floating around the bubbles in my bath.

When she stops humming, Mom says, "It's going to be all right, baby," to the water. "All all right," to the soapy mess she's wiping from my skin with her hand. "You hear?"

And it's as if the words just tumble out of her mouth and sit inside one of them bubbles—safe.

I open my mouth even though Mom always says swallowing soap will give me the runs. I watch the word bubble explode on my tongue. I swallow *It's going to be all right, baby, all all right.*

And like that, her words crawl right into me. They sit inside my head and wait. Like leftover chess pie in my Spider-Man lunch box for me to eat later when I'm super hungry.

I hate chess pie. The way even a teeny bite won't just be on my tongue. It crumbles like ants running on sand, tickling my tongue.

"Flaky," Mom calls it. "Nothing like chess pie, right?"

right?

Sometimes, if I repeat words enough times, they stick to the inside of my mouth like the sweet bits of Mom's chess pie.

The words gum up like glue, for later, when I need to throw them up.

Mom is picking my hair slowly and talking between the scrapes of the metal edges against my scalp. "You're—such—a—good—girl. My—Mapalo—such—a—beautiful—girl."

good girl.

beautiful girl.

It's supposed to teach me not to shout when a tooth of the comb snaps a coil loose. I'm supposed to stay real quiet because Dad's sleeping off his shift, and "he needs his rest." So I'm not supposed to squirm around till Mom's done and is patting the afro into place.

But see, it's also the morning after Halloween, and Mom won't let me carry my pack of Sour Patch Kids for snack time.

"That stuff'll rot your mouth," she says, pinching her face ugly. "And besides, I packed a slice of chess pie for you, Mapalo," Mom tells my head. "Ni favorite yako."

The whole time she's talking, I'm whining, "No, I want." 'Cause I want the whole scary-pumpkin-face bag of trick-or-treating instead of a slice of anything. Even when she's done combing, I keep whining. Even as she pats the tiny little hairs into a flat patch. As she says, "Come on, naiwe," and brings a round mirror to my front. "Big girls don't cry."

Big girls don't cry.

I watch my reflection try to pull the snot back into my nose.

At drop-off, I'm waving at Mom 'cause it feels like a recital, all the kids waving, all the moms waving back.

Someone else's mom asks mine which wave is hers with a little nod.

Mom grins. It's that all-her-teeth smile of hers that presses her eyes into sideways letter l's and writes wrinkles on her nose.

"The dimpled one," she says. "That's my daughter!"

She means to say it's beautiful, this smile of mine, 'cause it's the only thing I borrowed from her face.

dimpled…daughter!

In the waiting area, Sophia points at the booger before I lick it into my mouth again and pull my mask up.

She says, "Crybabyboogerface!" in her highest outside voice and starts to laugh.

I taught her that, you know? Back when Miss Steele first pushed our desks together.

Back when outside was still summer, even though our whiteboard was plastered with burnt-orange paper leaves.

Back when Sophia kept saying, "I just want my momma," under her breath like a little baby who didn't have all her words yet. I'm the one who said, "Crybabyboogerface!"

Afterward, Miss Steele had walked me straight to the naughty corner, pointed my head at the wall, and told me to "think about your words, young lady."

And I did.

Think-Cry-about-baby-your-booger-words-face, my mind sang.

Now the other kids' laughs fly everywhere. Bouncing inside my head with the morning bell.

When the lunch bell rings, everyone rushes out before me. Their voices climb all over each other before Miss Steele can say "Inside voices!" with her pointer finger shaking near her red lipstick.

Near the door, I swipe the box of Sour Nerds Sophia forgot on her desk. I spill the whole box into me and see my mouth rotting the shade of Lightning Lemon and Amped Apple. My chest starts to rattle, like I'm the box, my heart, so many pieces of candy I can't count them.

I smile.

But before I can swallow them, smash the evidence into itself, Miss Steele's hand is on my shoulder, spinning me around.

"Did you steal that, Paula?"

That's the only way my name can live in her mouth. *Paula.*

I close my eyes and listen to my hair. But everywhere has become this hushed quiet, like a big, grown-up secret.

In the cafeteria, the other students will be lining up now to collect their chicken nuggets and pears. Their voices almost reach us, like a faraway drum.

"If you do it again—"

do it again

My eyes flutter open and search her face.

Her eyes have bulged all wide now. As if maybe she is very afraid.

My insides shake softly, like Miss Steele's pointer finger would out in the hallway.

But my outside just stares at her nose. There it is, in the same exact place, with its exclamation point mole at the red tip. No, *itsokay* wrinkles like Moms or nothing.

"You know what happens to little girls who steal?" she says.

little girls . . . steal?

Says, "They get sent to jail, you know!"

jail, you know!

All the candy sweetness corrodes on my tongue, and the sweet-and-sour river slips down my throat.

I nod at Miss Steele and stuff her words into the same spot as *good* and *beautiful* and *dimpled . . . daughter.*

FERAL CHILDREN

> *Iri ndi maaké sikugwa.*
> Who keeps close to her mother does not fall.
>
> —Chewa proverb

I have bumped into an old, familiar scar again. In my chest, the pain blooms as sharp as a fresh wound, gaping.

A broken curfew; another missing Blackboard assignment; the iPhone I'd just confiscated; and my ex reneging on his "Daddy'll visit soon, Yanko" have conspired against me.

Now, bruises from all the times my daughter and I have sucked teeth at each other are exposed.

My once upon-a-little-girl vertigoes into a blur. In her place, a skinnier me, twenty-four years younger, cuts me a look. "I hate you," she seethes.

I stumble—at once foundling and vilomah.

Outside Yanko's bedroom door, I slide to the floor and hunt my mind for ways to kill the ache of making my womblove cry again. I find, instead, my mother's just-out-of-reach embrace. This glitch in my throat is me, twelve again. It's me gulping down sobs while "Bad by Myself" blasts from the radio. My father's fists against Mami's jaw harmonize with the base and her strangled screams. For a maddening beat, I leap back into July 1994, split seconds before Mami's body succumbed to my father's temper and made a feral child of me. In the gut of this old memory, Mami's lipstick bleeds red with her blood, staining her gums. But the apparition of her smile pacifies my desolation a little.

My daughter twists in her bed, craving her lullaby—the blue light of her phone. Slowly, Yanko's breath simmers down. Snores rise from the ashes of her sobbing and sit with me in the strained quiet.

Rising, I pry her door open and inch my way to her bed. Her eyes flutter but stay closed. "I'm sorry," I whisper.

AM-E-RI-CA

Mulendo ni jumi.
A traveler is dew.
—Tumbuka proverb

Outside the embassy, the man in front of us tells Mama that all she needs to do to get the visa is "look the white man in his eyes."

What if he is older? is what I would ask him because you're not supposed to look your elders in the eye, even if they shout, *Look at me!*

But Mama asks him, "Enhe, and you, how do you know?"

"My sista, trust me." He slaps his chest. "To those Americans"—with his head, he points at the glass door shielding the interview room from us—"disrespectful, it is the same as honesty."

"Jesus!" Mama exclaims, clapping. "Brother, have you yourself been to America?"

He rubs a sparse mustache and looks at the ceiling, where a ball of light in the center glares back. "Well, I got my bachelor's from the great American Central University."

"Enhe," Mama whispers. The clap that follows it is soft. "You're blessed," she declares.

"Here is my number," he says, handing her a business card. "Maybe we'll meet. You know, in America."

Mama feels the paper between her index and thumb. "In America," she whispers.

Inside, Mama keeps her hand fisted around mine while we wait for the voice behind the small window to shout "Next!"

Everyone, even Mr. America, has gone ghost-quiet. The visa interview room is a shuffle of papers, fingers against keyboard and beeping screens.

So far, it is exactly as I remember, except for my toes, dancing at the end of my shoes, shifting my body from foot to foot and when Mama's instruction was for me to stay still and silent. "Mama," I'm trying to whisper, but all this unfilled space is making it a shout.

Mama peels her fingers off slow, like maybe she'll let me dash across the tile to the glowing *TOILET* flashing against a bone-white door. But when she snaps them back, we're glued together. Peanut-butter-to-roof-of-mouth tight and doesn't even look down.

The button on my dress is pressed to the spot where my belly button bulges now, shooting stabs of pain where normally I feel nothing. "Mama," I beg.

Beneath the air cons breathing cold air onto our heads, my arms are a thick film of goose pimples, but my palm is slick. I smell Mama's sweat beneath the aroma of Blue Magic. Usually, it's just the grease I smell. Unless she's afraid. And what I know is, Mama is afraid of unchained barking dogs and nothing else. A gleaming V-shaped keloid below her elbow marks her terror spot. I sweep the room with my eyes, even though there's nothing new to see. Everything is white except the people on this side of three tiny windows, all of them clasping manila folders and passports, whisper-talking, but no dogs.

"I really need to go."

Mama keeps her eyes ahead, digs her nails into the back of my hand, but otherwise pretends she can't hear me.

Mr. America has started shouting "Why, why?" at the voice behind the glass. "I have all the documentation right here! You didn't even look. Just look!" He's scrambling for papers when a guard steps in front of him and grabs his arm. The man grows quiet. His big shoulders stop heaving, but the soles of his shoes squeak long and loud against the tile as he is dragged out of the room.

"Next!"

Mama's nails are still digging into my skin as she pulls me forward. Like maybe she suspects that I've already forgotten her "Behave, Julie!" from earlier and will escape for the toilet, like last time.

"And you're a nurse?" the voice on the other side of the window asks.

Mama is wearing her uniform and the tights with the tiny ladders crawling up her calves. Her cap is sitting like a crown in front of her puff. *Sister Laika Maiwanga*, says her badge pinned to her breast pocket. "Yes," she replies.

The voice pulls out an "Okaaay?" like maybe it thinks Mama's uniform is just a dress, sewn for her by the tailor at the market. Like me on Careers Day wearing head to toe doctor's blue and telling everyone I am Dr. Maiwanga, not Julie.

"Have you been to the US before?" it asks.

Mama's nails scrape the back of my hand, quickening my dance. "No, sir," she says. Each time the voice asks a question, she repeats the motion, squeezes my hand, and says, "Yes, sir. No, sir."

"Have you had a visa application denied before?"

Scratch. Squeeze. "Yes." The *s* wobbles, like me, just before I cry.

"Why?" Papers shuffle on the other side of the window.

"I don't know, sir." A lie.

After the last *no*, Mama cried as soon as she took her seat in the back of the congested minibus all the way home. In her prayer that night, she accused the Devil of trying to withhold happiness from us. She even blamed Grandfather's youngest wife, Lute, for being an ugly witch. But Mama stopped sniffling when she got to "No weapon formed against me shall prosper, Amen!"

"Okay," says the voice.

Squeeze.

The voice waits a long moment before speaking. "Ookaay."

Squeeze.

"Ms. Maiwanga. Your visa has been granted. You and your daughter go on and enjoy your holiday."

Outside, the air hot and singing, a bus whizzes past the *DO NOT PARK HERE* signage in the grass and screeches to a stop where it ends. A conductor slides the door open, hangs on its hinges, and shouts "Mukwela!" at no one in particular. Mr. America has just stomped across Kabulonga Road. He slams his Pajero's door closed and speeds off.

Mama presses her hands to her chest, the way she sometimes cradles my head when I wake up from a bad dream crying. "We're going to America, Julie!"

"Am-e-ri-ca." I taste each syllable and give Mama the smile, which everyone says is just like hers, just with two dimples instead of one.

"Didn't I tell you? Julie," Mama says. "The Devil is a liar!" She punches the air and spins around.

This was our fourth application. The first *yes* granted at the cost of Mama pawning everything in our house. The only thing left is the Foam-King mattress, which bore the yellowed stains of each of my nightmares, crooked maps wiping away the pretty blue of roses on the cover. Uncleanable, no matter how many times Mama scrubbed. Every morning that she made me drag it outside to dry on the patch of grass next to the veranda, the neighborhood children pointed and sang "Chisusu!" at me.

"Do we have to hang things outside in America?" I ask.

She laughs. Her face is an outline against the sun, sharp dark lines where her forehead, nose, lips, and chin should be. "No," she says when she looks back down at me. "In America, Julie, they have washing machines, dryers, everything."

"And toys?" I ask between giggles.

Mama grips my shoulders and squeezes. "Julie. Don't tell anyone?" Her eyes bulge at me in silent warning. She darts them from the guards standing watch at the embassy gate and then back down at me.

"Let me go," I groan, shrugging uselessly. I'm already picturing myself prancing along Lui road all afternoon, swinging my American-visa passport more than I would a thigh bone after a chicken lunch.

OBLIGATIONS TO THE WOUNDED

"You never know what evil plans someone has over us, ka? This is a secret, you hear!"

"But what about saying bye to my friends."

"But what about saying bye to my friends." She makes a poor imitation of me. Her mouth is folded into a grimace, which pushes her red lipstick out of the black line of pencil lining her lips.

She straightens herself to her full height, something she does a lot now that I'm up to her armpits. "I said, 'Do. Not. Tell. Anyone.' Wanvela!"

I swivel my head, up a little and then down, enough for her to accept it as a nod. She lets me go.

My body sways a little, a wind blows, my thighs grow warm. When I part them a little, wetness trickles down, sticky and hot. I close my eyes and listen to the *drip-drip* onto the neat little flat stones.

WHISPER DOWN THE LANE

Mu nwana u li mumu au koni ku tuba nda.
One finger cannot kill a louse.

—Lozi proverb

We watched quietly as One absorbed his words. She was perched at her desk, where chalk dust fell from the blackboard and coated her face white. Later, she'd swear he said, "I stepped in a mouse to make my tea this morning." Complete nonsense, but some words must have gotten tangled up in his enormous mustache. Perhaps his lisp distorted them, or maybe she was distracted by the stripped mulberry branch swinging in his hand. We couldn't decide which.

We remember her smiling when she tilted her head right and tried to guess what words lingered behind her hands cupped as they were around her mouth. She spilled a whisper into the next girl, who told the next, and then the next.

At the very back of the class, Fifty-Seven fidgeted in her chair, anxiously waiting. Through the broken door behind her, the jacaranda flowers floated in silently to stain the concrete floor purple around her Bata shoes. The wind, meanwhile, carried the melodies of choir practice and splintered piano chords from the music room across the dusty schoolyard into Fifty-Seven's ear.

When finally, Fifty-Seven sprang to her feet and reported, "He scratched crap and sucked fleas!" We guffawed. We tossed our heads back in the sure way of our mothers when they swapped gossip over clothes wires and blood hibiscus brush. For an instant, the room was a blur of moving lips as We shouted what We'd said and quarreled over who had misheard.

He cracked the whip across Three's table and smirked when he missed her fingertips, and she jumped.

"I said, 'I stopped at my mother's house this morning for a sip of tea.' But that's how gossip works. Lies driven by lies!"

We swallowed our chuckles, even though his *s* sprayed his saliva everywhere, catching dust motes before descending to the floor. "Yes, sir!" We muttered.

"What's the lesson here, girls?" He scanned our pimply faces, row after tight row of trimmed afros, nodding, silent.

A fevered look seized the brown of his eyes, searing them charcoal in an instant. "Whoever keeps his mouth and his tongue keeps himself out of trouble," he said, but proceeded still to lash us.

"For not paying attention," he said to One. He slammed her into the table, pressed her new breasts onto the cracked wood by keeping one hand firmly on the small of her back. He was leaning so close to her that his flared nostrils must've stung with the peppermint notes in her soap beneath the smell of sweat rising from the pit stains on her uniform.

"For lying," to Thirty-Six, who was already sobbing. A river of mucus crawled from her nose into her open mouth before the stick even landed on her buttock.

"This will teach you girls not to throw talk around anyhow, enh? Focus on your books!"

He left her there whimpering and staggered out, wagging his whip, while We waited for a small forever.

It was Five who started the train, then passed it on to Six, then Seven. But when he returned, trailed by the stench of nicotine, We were still glued to our assigned spots.

We pretended to focus on the diagrams of fat grasshoppers in the science textbooks spread across our desks and waited.

"There was a lot of noise in here while I was outside," he announced—a lie as filthy as the yellow stains on his teeth.

The only sound he walked into was the scraping of metal against concrete as someone crouched over the next desk to spread the word. We were going to "leach him a reason."

He did not wait for our "Welcome back, sir!" to simmer down.

He reached for Thirty-Eight's arm, but she grabbed his wrist and snatched the whip.

When he gasped, his terror was the hush in our mothers' voices when their husbands returned staggering, angry, eager-fisted, and hungry.

We traced the steps back to the last word of the plan, swapped nods and sly grins. We shot a final look at the gaping door for any witnesses.

None.

Together, We roared as Thirty-Eight cracked the stick against his balding head.

His yelp was our laughter—thin, long, hollow, strong.

We surged forward.

And when We laughed, it was the joy of our mothers when the neighborhood thief was finally caught. In our minds, it was him squeezed into a tire liner, plummeting down a dusty hill.

We thrashed until he was scampering, arms reaching, body catching, scurrying out of the classroom.

SPEAKING ENGLISH

<blockquote>
Akebo kalababa.
Words itch.
—**Bemba proverb**
</blockquote>

Mama and I stood together facing three little rectangular buildings.
All of them were painted white with square windows in a straight line,
side by side like the cornrows on my head. I counted them out loud and
told Mama my findings, as though she wasn't looking at the very same
thing. "Ten squares!"

"Hmm" was all she said because, as she'd been telling me the whole
way here, "We are late."

I could count as high as all my fingers, name all seven colors that
painted the sky after a rainstorm, and spell my name, K-A-T-E-U-L-E,
with my mouth and on a piece of paper, but still didn't know how to tell
the time. That must have been why I found it hard to understand how
we could possibly be late. Above us, a green flag hung flaccid next to
the school sign. Behind us, cars crawled in traffic, and above us, the sky
was still gray, waiting for the sun to warm it up.

"Crap," Mama said, frowning at her wrist again. "We are so late." She said the *so* long, in the breathless tone she used to call me when she was annoyed. *Sooo.*

I wanted to ask her how we could have been late when we'd trot-walked the whole way from home. When the sky was still black as we stepped onto the veranda, and the fading moonlight was still glittering in the beads of water scattered across the grass in our front yard. But from the way Mama's eyebrows were bunched together, as she tapped her feet and smoothed the front of her shirt in between knocking her folded knuckles against the little red gate, I knew to hold the question on my tongue for when she was smiling and not stretching words.

The gate squeaked and swung open. A woman stepped out. She had big hair with a fringe tucked into her eyebrows and a skirt so puffy I wanted to bury my head in it. The woman grinned. "Good morning!" she said to Mama. "Welcome to Little Angels Nursery School."

She wasn't tapping her heels against the paved entryway or bunching her eyebrows together, but Mama still said, "I'm so sorry we are late. This is my daughter." Her *sorry* was stretched out. *Soorry.* She handed the woman a piece of paper.

Mama stooped down to my height, licked her thumb, and wiped the side of my mouth with it. "Be a good girl today." She straightened back up, and nudged me toward the grinning woman's poofy skirt and spun around to continue her trot-walk to teach her own students at Luanshya Boys Secondary School. She'd have to walk the same way we'd just come, over the bridge framed by trees so tall they bent over and nearly touched at the top, past our house, to the other side of Luanshya.

The woman turned her grin to me. "Welcome!"

I was supposed to say "Thank you very much" and curtsy my respect for this elder as I did all others. But there was already too much to remember, like which one was my book bag, black and worn at the corners; its contents, a lunch box of fresh chapati and an avocado paste, two pencils, a pink eraser and a sharpener.

She offered her hand to me, and when I did, it smelled like Mama. Like the white flesh of a coconut after you cracked open the brown skin. I squeezed her palm three times. But it wasn't Mama, so she didn't squeeze back the *I love you*. We strolled past a swing, a seesaw, and a slide, all of them silver with brown patches that looked like a rash. The hallway was decorated with pictures next to the letters of the alphabet. I grinned my gummy grin because I knew them all. We stopped at a red door with a picture of a pink smiling baby where a hum of little voices rose up and down on the other side. There, the woman turned to me and said, "Don't speak Bemba, speak English."

Mama had already taught me how to hold my pencil so that I didn't tear into the paper when I traced numbers into it. She had reminded me to raise my hand and ask the teacher first if I needed to go to the toilet and eat only the food she packed into the plastic box, even though she knew I hated avocados unless they had sugar and Cowbell powdered milk mixed in. At home, we spoke mostly Bemba, so I fumbled with the instruction, opening my mouth and then closing it. Mama used English only when new people were around.

Was the language painted onto my lips like lipstick? Had Mama failed to wipe it completely off with her finger before she left? With the back of my hand, I wiped my mouth.

The woman frowned. "That is our only rule," she said. "Do you understand?"

Yes, I nodded.

She said, "Good," then opened the red door to a class of faces that stopped talking the exact moment we appeared.

The school had other rules, of course, written in white chalk on a blackboard next to the Headmistress's Office. Our teacher, always in poofy skirts and kitten heels, who eventually introduced herself as Miss Lucy, read them to us every day until we knew them like all twenty-six letters in the alphabet. But it was easy to remember to be silent during classes with our forefingers pressed against our mouths. We could take turns grazing the back of our legs on the metal slide at break time because we stood behind the little ladder in a line from shortest to tallest. But tongues are wild things, once they learn that they can move without our control. Tongues writhe whichever way they please. Ours had already wrapped themselves around the Bemba speech pattern, rejected every *R* in the English language, leaving us fumbling at the end of the school day when we all had to chorus "See you tomorrow!" to our teacher. The last word sputtered out of our mouths, a deliberate murmur, intoned in a collective half whisper.

I have been speaking English now for twenty-five years, properly for twenty. At first, as a performance, for my mother's friends, who came over every Sunday after church. If I said "I am fine, thank you, auntie. How are you?" in response to their greeting, I knew they would take the tumblers of diluted Mazoe with those jealous grins, which made Mama lean back into the sofa, waiting for them to say, "My, she speaks so well!"

But now it comes first. English. Even when I meet strangers. *Why then are my fingers wound so tight around the straps of my backpack? Why does it feel like each digit is vibrating as rapidly as my heart?* I pat myself down, inspect myself as Mama would if she were leaving me here herself. My black pumps are spotless; there is so little dirt here it's a wonder that anything grows. My legs tingle against the wind, hairless for the first time in my life after my roommate exclaimed this morning, "Oh. My. God. You don't shave your legs?" And then insisted on showing me how. I tapped my hair, straightened, and slicked down under a palmful of gel into a skinny ponytail. But even without my afro, I feel myself sticking out like a full stop penciled in too thick on a blank white page. They shuffle past me, in and out of the swinging glass doors in front of me.

"Phew," I say, probably too loudly because "I Wanna Be Down" is pulsing through my headphones, set to the highest volume. Nothing like the husk of Brandy's voice early in the morning. The word escapes my mouth in a big puff of air, forming a thin white cloud before it disappears. As my music winds down, the crowd begins to dwindle around me. I release my fingers and shake the nerves from my shoulders and then through my feet as I take step after step toward my first class. This is why I had sat the TOEFL examination, paid for extra data on my phone to sit with my laptop at night and write, revise, then rewrite essay after essay about why I was the right candidate for this university, this class, this scholarship.

I navigate the maze, counting the numbers on the doors until I am at the right one, open it, and pad into the class, massive and obnoxious. I take the first open seat I spot at the back and pull out my notebook and pencil case, ready to take notes. But when the professor, standing at a podium in front, speaks, she asks for our names instead. My heart-beat spikes again. I was prepared to answer why I had chosen a master's in public administration or why I was taking her course on public policy analysis. The answers to both were that I wanted to use the skills I acquired to return to my HR position in the Ministry of General Education. Leaving the part about the job having nothing to do with public policy unsaid because what did it matter? Mama would, after all, be waiting, on the other end of my graduation in two years, to show me off on Sundays. Her daughter, with the degree from America. My turn comes after forty-nine others have spoken, and the professor fixes her gaze in my direction. I rise, clear my throat, and say, "Good morning, my name is Kateule Kanyanta."

She scans her paper, looking for my name on her list, I presume. My heart slows down, air returning to my lungs as my bottom finds my seat again.

"Ah yes," she says. "Can I call you Kate instead?"

No, I think. *The e in my name isn't even silent.* I want to repeat my name, slower, even though she is talking faster than her lips seem to be moving. *Ka-te-wu-lay, the way I've just heard my classmates intone theirs.* Hailee with two *e*'s. Sarah with an *h*. Jaxon with an *x*. But then, how do I say "Kateule," as in "kateule imbale," as in "clear away the dishes."

She blinks at me and takes off her glasses. The other students shift in their seats and stare.

"Yes," I say.

IT WILL BE BEAUTIFUL AGAIN

Kubucha uleta tunji.
Tomorrow brings many things.
—Tonga proverb

1. Kaapa

It wasn't always like this. Stuck in a metal prison disguised as a hospital bed. There was a time when your throat thirsted for cold Fanta and sizzling hot vitumbuwa straight out of the frying pan. It wasn't always tablet after massive tablet pushed down with sugary milk in a plastic cup stinking of leftover detergent. Before the sickness burned your blood into flames, it was beautiful.

Remember? When you wore too much powder over the film of glycerine and wiping away the little brown river sliding down the side of your face as the sun beat down on Lusaka, you would moan about the humidity: "Oh my God!" You'd fan yourself with a flimsy handkerchief, its white cotton now muddied with your melted makeup. "If it's this hot in April, we will have to walk naked in October." You'd guffaw. That magnificent laugh, seeping between your red-red lips, spilling into everyone's ear, forcing their heads to turn in your direction. Remember, Beenzu, when you could slip your dainty feet into polka-dot heels, which you'd bought for a steal in a pile of salaula at Soweto Market. Your shoes clicked through long hospital corridors, into wards just like this one with baskets filled with a dying relative's cravings—Jolly Juice, bananas, big jars of strawberry yogurt.

Did you even glance at the Project SIDA posters plastered to every tree trunk on your bus rides? Did you think the big red plus over the skeleton would one day hang over your own head? When the doctor said "Tuberculosis," did he also mention how quickly it would slither into the rest of your body? Sucking the flesh from your thighs, chest, and face?

No.

Which man had left more than the stink of sex in your two-bedroom flat in Kabwata when they left?

Torn-boxer-brief-Mwansa or forgetful-Mwale, who let you discover by bumping into him, his wife, and three children buying groceries in Shoprite that he was married?

No.

Maybe it was Nyambe, a secondary-school English teacher like you, whose "I will marry you soon" never came.

You grind your teeth together and dart your eyes around the room, searching for a visible target for your dizzying rage since none of those men have been to see you.

What if it was Chipego's father? When you saw him last, he sweated on top of you in a musty lodge behind the university.

What if—?

You gulp air.

What if it was you spreading it every time you flung your head back, moaned as your thighs opened in front of you?

No!

Your eyes land on the voile curtains the same color as the sky, then the window, gaping wide, allowing chatter, chirping, pollen, and fresh air into your hospital room. The droning TV, as usual, draws them with its regurgitation of *international news*: Clinton and Blair on BBC and CNN. The door is closed, but to your left, someone stirs—your grandmother.

"Oh!" Kaapa claps. "You are awake." She fiddles with the porridge bowl, smells like groundnuts and butter, then the bottle of pills and adjusts herself in the seat so that she can reach your mouth with the spoon.

You scowl and blink back hot tears.

"Akaka, kolya, please." Kaapa begs you to eat. The meal was once your favorite, cooked with mealie meal and milk first thing in the morning before you went to school. But you aren't seven anymore. The supermarkets and tuntembas now stock sliced bread, Buttercup margarine, and mixed-fruit jam in loud red cans. Only, the sores in your throat won't allow anything but porridge through to your stomach. So you drop your chin to your chest and keep your gaze on the spoon between your grandmother's wrinkled fingers, feeding you until the bowl is empty.

"Enhe, good," she says, patting your head gently and fluffing your pillow. "Now you have the strength to take your medicine." Another chore for your tongue. Even when the pills are crushed and diluted into the water for you to drink.

You nod, willing the strength to return. You muster a whisper, "Where is she?"

"Ati nzi?" Kaapa asks, pulling her eyebrows together.

"Chipego." You cough out your daughter's name. "Where is she?"

Her answer is to lather Vaseline into the cracks on your lips. "Pumuna," she insists. "Even just a little rest will do you some good."

Does she really believe that? That rest will take away sores in your throat, your fever and swollen groin. She stands to tuck the starched sheets around you. You want to claw out and scream, *No!* You want to slap the toothy smile off her face. Kaapa pushes hair from your forehead, rubs talcum powder into your chest, and wobbles to the other side of the bed to take her seat. She picks up her hymnbook and sings you a song: "*Sena moona, kamu buka. Sena moona, kamu buka.*"

The melody pacifies the flames in your head and reduces you to the infant Kaapa could once swing over her back and wrap into a chitenge, quelling your screams when your mother was away until you slept, instead of a thirty-two-year-old woman, a high school English teacher, a mother of a ten-year-old girl.

Chipego.

Your sight grows foggy, your face relaxed, your lids fluttering open and shut, head swaying to the tune.

"*Sena moona, kamu buka. Sena moona, kamu buka.*"

Are you sleeping? Wake up. Are you sleeping? Wake up.

2. Baama

The lullaby carries you to a dream, flinging you back ten years into the past.

It's 1987 again—a humid Friday with the unfulfilled promise of rain. You have yelled until your voice is raw, wobbled down the narrow corridor, naked, gripping the walls for something that will pull the pain from you, yet still, the waves continue to come, longer and stronger each time, gripping your back and then your stomach, tying it up into knots, like fikuti braided too tight in a little girl's head. Any other Friday, you'd have been seated on the banks of Goma Lakes. You'd be in Bible study with other students from the Christian Centre at the University of Zambia, where you should be completing your bachelor's degree. Instead, you are here. Yelling "I'm dying!" and "Help me!"

An irate nurse charges at you. "Chongo iwe!"

It's the fourth warning she's giving you. She pressed a plump finger against her mouth. "Some of your friends who have already done the work are trying to sleep." She grabs you by the arm and leads you back to the bed.

"Please, sister," you beg. "Check again."

She rolls her eyes. "Last time," she says, snapping on a fresh pair of gloves. "Ready?"

No. But you nod.

Her face grows tender, showing where the lines have aged it— around her mouth, creeping from the corners of her eyes, on the bridge of her nose. "I know," she says, taking your other arm with less force. "But it will be over soon."

You howl when she digs her fingers into you.

"Try and reserve your energy now, enh? You will need it to bring your baby into the world." She cocks her head to one side as if she wants you to answer, and for a fleeting moment, you absently wonder why the white rectangular cap on top of her patted down afro doesn't move.

"I—I—" you stutter. "I want my mother."

The nurse smiles. "I know," she whispers.

If not for the searing ache in your core, you'd purse your lips or click your tongue. What does she know about Baama? Or her anger if she knew you'd been sent back from your teacher training at St. Josephs because you were pregnant and unmarried? Her tiny body would implode. She'd grab your ear and shout, "What will I do with you, Beenzu?"

She would remind you of the time you were sixteen. She had to go against her Christian beliefs to pay a ng'anga to concoct a brew to turn the baby inside you into menstrual blood. She would tell you how she had risked her reputation among her sisters, friends, and the other wives whose daughters didn't return from boarding school carrying pregnancies along with their food trunks and schoolbooks only for you to do it again.

"Shall I swallow you and carry you around in my stomach forever?" she'd lament, reminding you how hard it had been for her. Widowed in her thirties and raising daughters alone. For what? "Only for you to be so troublesome, always dropping out of trees as if you were a boy who had grown up in the village instead of modern cities like Mufulira and Ndola and Lusaka."

You imagine you would hang your head and let your mind meander into some distant place. Probably Achebe's Umuofia, in a front-row seat to a wrestling match, until Baama's rant ended with "Try to be like your little sister, enh!"

Yet as the nurse instructs you to hold your ankles and keep your knees spread apart, you crave Baama's fingers rubbing your back. You want Baama to wipe the sweat dripping out of your braids onto your face. You want her steady voice to remind you that challenges were a test of character, to count the adversity you have surmounted so far. Like being born prematurely just in time for Zambia's independence and surviving alone in the hospital, feeding on a bottle of breast milk she had pumped by hand and stored in a neighbor's fridge for a week before your parents could bring it to you.

You wish it was her voice saying "Push!" and "Rest!" or that she was about to cut you "to give the baby's head more room."

Baama should be in this cramped ward with you, witnessing her first granddaughter making her loud entrance into the world just as the humidity finally relents and makes way for the rain.

When the news reaches Baama, and she strolls into your ward, there is no rage in her tight smile. You are no longer worthy of that even. She has boiled the anger, simmered it down into clipped reminders of this latest mistake—a living, growing thing.

"Is *this* what my granddaughter is wearing," your mother would say on her visits. Clicking her tongue and shaking her head. "She looks so thin." She'd hand her a box of biscuits.

Relief is the split second when the dream disappears back into your mind.

You wake before you remember where you are.

Your eyes flicker to the white walls, white floors, and white door.

Baama's face peering into yours.

Never mind that you'd been pining for her as much as you had been for your daughter. Forget missing the way she cooks kidney beans, adding the onions and an extra scoop of oil at the very end. Ignore the warmth spreading in your chest at the scent of her cocoa butter lotion, forcing your nostrils wide, showing their open joy at anything other than the stench of bleach and methylated spirit that waft through every hall of the hospital except the ablution block.

You harden your jaw. "Is Chipego coming?"

Baama laughs the laugh you used to laugh. Taking up all the empty spaces.

"God is good. Say something else." She places your palm into hers.

They are the same brown of the earth after it rains, with a big mole where her forefinger meets her thumb. "We haven't heard your voice all week, my baby. Thank God you're healing. Talk to me."

She won't stop talking long enough to let you.

The phrase is stolen. *My baby*. Stolen from you.

It's something you sprinkled on Chipego to make her smile. When she brought back a report card filled with As and the number one written in the slot for the position in her class. For when she remembered to wash the plates after lunch before running back into the street to play. For when she didn't drench her hair in the bathroom, right after you paid K1000 for it to be blow-dried while she wailed in the salon. For the times she remembered to touch the floor with her knees when she served nsima for her uncles. For when she said "Maa" when any adult called her instead of her usual disrespectful "Enh?"

Your heart cracks as you remember when the saying first hooked itself into you. You were eight, hiding in your family munda, among maize stalks, having braided each cob instead of pulling weeds out of the dirt like your cousins were doing. When Baama approached you and surveyed your handiwork, she didn't pinch your cheeks or drag you out of the field by the arms. She beamed at you and said, "Well done, my baby! You can braid now." It was her saying after all, not yours.

You pry your hand out of hers and look at Kaapa. "Water." You cup your fingers around an invisible glass and bring it to your mouth.

Baama leaps to her feet to place the plastic bottle to your lips. She holds your head up with her other hand and then wipes the dribble from your neck with the sleeve of her pink chiffon shirt.

You want to gurgle it and spit in her face.

What could possibly be keeping her so busy at home? Wiping her trays of the royal wedding? Arranging flowers for the occasional customer?

You squint at her performance, grimace, swallow spit, water, and pride.

3. Chipego

Just then, Chipego bounces in, wearing her gray school uniform ripped on one side and covered in dust.

You swallow.

This is her second visit since you were admitted to the hospital over a month ago. Last time, she was bursting with stories. Who had done what at school last week, which games she was expert in and was now beating all the boys at. Unlike you, she hangs on the branches of the trees she climbs, dropping to the ground only when she wants to. She has your skinny legs but not the knocked knees. They carry her faster than yours ever did, winning races for her school where you'd quit halfway, pretending to faint—anything to not finish last. She had slaughtered a chicken, she'd told you, because the maid you hired right before this was too scared to do it. To prove that she was ready for her upcoming grade seven examinations, Chipego had memorized her current affairs. On her last visit, she recited them to you. "Princess Diana died on the thirty-first of August last year. I mean, 1997. Edith Nawakwi is the first female finance minister of Zambia."

Now your daughter just blinks at you, mouth agape.

"Come." You try your hardest not to sound as terrified as you are and give her a smile.

Chipego doesn't move.

Panic clamps itself around your neck.

Are you now invisible too?

An inaudible scream.

"Come, my baby."

You realize then that the room is filled with faces other than Kaapa's, Baama's, Chipego's, and your own. Cousins you haven't seen since your little sister threw her last lavish party for her three-year-old, jumping castle, three cakes, and all. Aunts who've been feuding with your mother for years hover close by, lips pursed and arms pushing their breasts into their chins. In the corner, your sister, Luyando, is peering over the heads of the others like she was forced to go to the zoo. With her long hair pinned back, stretching the skin on her face and arching her eyebrows, she looks like you once did.

Luyando clears her throat. "Sissy." Her cheeks burn red where the bleach has started peeling off her skin.

The aunties move aside, leaving just enough room between themselves for Luyando to glide through to the foot of your bed. She fiddles with her hoops, dabs rouge off the corners of her mouth, and settles her gaze on the hill on the blanket created by your feet.

"You know we are all praying for you."

Amen, the aunts chorus.

"In fact, atupaile."

You watch them close their eyes, press their palms together, and bow their heads. Luyando calls God every name but God.

On Sundays, it is *you* who boards a crammed minibus to Christ Ministries Church. It is *you* who drops to the floor, speaking tongues. Each week when the pastor asked people to welcome Jesus into their heart and come to the front. You test your last seven days: drank wine until you nodded off in a friend's room; gossiped about new mate's body odor. Each weekend you heeded your pastor's call. Luyando prefers to attend church once a month, as if she's reminding God that she's still there. When she ends her prayer with the sign of the cross, only then do you press your eyelids together while fisting your fingers into balls.

"Baama," you hear yourself say.

"Yes?"

Please leave Chipego and me alone for a minute, you signal with your eyes at your daughter still standing next to the door.

Baama's eyes glisten. She pats herself down and laugh-talks. "Let us give them some privacy."

Privacy? You'd cackle if you could. The doors into the house you grew up in didn't have any locks except the one to her bedroom and the pantry.

Kaapa huddles over a bucket of your belongings. Arranging and rearranging blankets over chitenges, socks, and underwear. She has not left your side since you were admitted. She's like a new mother watching her fledgling. As if you will stop breathing if she looks away.

"Kaapa. Please."

She nods and leads the train of women out. The women squeeze Chipego's shoulder, nudging her closer to your bed.

When the door closes, the girl sniffles and wipes her eyes.

"Chipego." Your voice trips. "My baby."

She shuffles first and then bolts toward you, burying her face in your chest. When she pulls away to look at you, you see she's lost her earrings again. There are specks of dirt in her loose puff.

"Mummy?" It's as if she's not sure it's you lying under the blankets.

Don't cry. Don't cry. Don't cry.

"Yes, baby. Ndime—It's me." You smell her hair, the familiar scent of Dax. Her eyes search your face, her thick brows disappearing into a V on her forehead.

"Mummy, please. Come back."

Here's the girl you'd raised alone. Your fearless child. She's been reduced to sobs in your arms, as though she's four again, wanting to follow you around, wailing when she's told no.

You sigh. "It will be fine. My baby?"

The question mark forms itself. It trails other questions behind it.

Who would remember to add mabisi to Chipego's samp?

What use had it been to teach her how to wash dirty dishes with just one bucket of water?

Would she enjoy the flaps of skin dangling between her legs which you'd insisted she pull for her future husband?

You know from Kaapa's hunched back, from your mother scurrying out of the room, from the flame of AIDS searing through your veins: you know you won't be going back home.

You try to meet her eyes, but the stupid things in the room keep drawing your gaze instead. Those impossibly blue curtains, a black bird perched on the branches of a tree outside, the boy and girl holding the coat of arms on the flashing image on the screen.

How do you cram a lifetime of lessons into one moment?

The things you should have said instead of teaching Chipego to sit with her legs closed, to wash her underwear in the bucket of bathwater, wring it dry, and hang it somewhere no one would see it.

"There will be bad days sometimes," you whisper. "But it will be beautiful again. Someday."

#BAILEYLIES

Ndadziwa kale adamanga nyumba yopanda khomo.
Who said "I know everything" built his house without a door.
—Chewa proverb

I type in Karen Bai— when the top suggestion gives me the person I am looking for.

Karen Bailey ✔ @KayTheAuthor
Humanitarian | Writer | Actress #EscapeFromRhodesia

An avatar of three toddlers of the help-starving-kids-in-Africa variety greets me. Their oversized, ripped T-shirts expose cracked shoulders and skinny necks. But for the gap-toothed grins, they could be one of those black-and-white pictures beneath headings for kwashiorkor and marasmus in my old science textbooks. A white arm loops around their shoulders, a French-tip-manicured hand rested on one shoulder.

One face for each of Karen's three titles, I think.

The header is a selfie of Karen, holding a Starbucks cup in one hand and a copy of *Escape from Rhodesia* in the other. The only thing missing from the book cover, an image of a flaming orange sky, is Pride Rock's outline with one of the children dangling in Rafiki's hands.

> 📌 **Pinned Tweet**
> **Karen Bailey** ✔ @KayTheAuthor • Apr 22, 2016 12:46 am
> • from Portland, Oregon • Twitter for iPhone
> Buy my book, *Escape from Rhodesia*, <u>HERE</u>.

I roll my eyes, slam my copy of the book closed onto my pillow, and type a reply, which I fully expect to be ignored. The blue light from my screen is the only light in the room. I live in the part of Lusaka that ZESCO sees fit to allot the heaviest burden of the countrywide load shedding. Electricity hasn't been restored since the last power outage two days ago, and the blue from my screen is the only light in the room. I feel the bed for my laptop, still warm from when I turned it off to do my little research using my phone. The air is too hot for me to keep my windows closed, and I lean away from my mosquito net, closer to the bed. They whine anyway, right by my head.

> **Tafara Zulu** @TruthTeller1 Replying to @KayTheAuthor A book based in Africa? I'm in! Zambia or Rhodesia, though?

Karen Bailey ✔ @KayTheAuthor responds before I tap out of her page and scroll down to the #RIPPrince tweets or rants accompanying pictures of Arthur's fist.

I pat the screen for a beat. Deciding on what to say next.

> **Karen Bailey** ✅ @KayTheAuthor Replying to @TruthTeller1
> LOL. Zambia! Used to be Northern Rhodesia, FYI.

Ha! Will you just listen to this muzungu? There she is with her pouting red lips, pale skin, and matching hair, trying to teach *me* my own country's history. I suck my teeth, type, delete, and finally settle on *Oh, wow, okay! Would love to interview you*, after reading it aloud to myself.

While I wait, I picture her fingernails clicking through my page, deciding if the *Journalist@Makani | Opinions are my own* in my bio makes me worthy of any more of her attention. The second part is still true. At least, that's what I keep telling myself. And the first, well, that will be true again once Karen says yes. Once I turn these screenshots into an article for the newspaper, I'll reverse the demotion my stupid boss had called a "realignment. Realigned from field reporter to the Mulomo, classified ads editor. Imagine it! As if proofing those endless witch doctor ads—*Doctor Mutototo! Come for penis enlargement, bring back lost lovers, fix money problems, cure AIDS*—was the job equivalent of the soulmate I've been waiting for.

> **Karen Bailey** ✅ @KayTheAuthor Replying to @TruthTeller1
> OFC! Anything 2 spotlight this super important story.
> #EscapefromRhodesia
> **Tafara Zulu** @TruthTeller1 Replying to @KayTheAuthor
> ~~😂But Rhodesia doesn't exist as country anymore!~~
> **Tafara Zulu** @TruthTeller1 Replying to @KayTheAuthor
> Why Zambia?

> **Karen Bailey** ✔ @KayTheAuthor Replying to @TruthTeller1
> GOSH! So much suffering in the world & I've always wanted
> 2b part of the solution, y'know? #EscapefromRhodesia

I feel the muscles in my face tighten as I swap Twitter for Wiki-
pedia. There, I'm reminded that, yes, this is the same Karen Bailey of
Milling Castle. A whole fucking castle! Owned by her parents in a
country I could only imagine seeing on the other side of a visa interview and a plane ride I will never afford.

With that, my thoughts flash to my parents' house. Two bedrooms
in Libala for all six of their children and every orphaned cousin whom
my mother took upon herself to adopt. I remember our single beds,
mine shared with the cousin who hadn't stopped urinating until long
after her fourteenth birthday and my youngest sister, who spun around
the bed all night. I shift in my bed and decide as I unclench my teeth
that I have to get my old job back. Have to get this story, because I
cannot go back to my old bed, no matter what.

I press the letters on my screen harder than I need to. Type, type,
type, delete, delete, delete, and replace, replace, replace.

> **Tafara Zulu** @TruthTeller1 Replying to @KayTheAuthor ~~SO~~
> ~~MUCH TO UNPACK!~~
> **Tafara Zulu** @TruthTeller1 Replying to @KayTheAuthor Did
> you feel you were able to help?
> **Karen Bailey** ✔ @KayTheAuthor Replying to @TruthTeller1
> No spoilers! I was just bewitched by the people, & obvi the
> language. I met this little girl: just a beautiful creature, TBH.

Poor thing could have been my own, the way she just wor-
shipped me! #EscapefromRhodesia
Tafara Zulu @TruthTeller1 Replying to @KayTheAuthor
~~Worship? WORSHIP?! 😠 Is she in your avatar?~~

I zoom in on the picture, examine each tiny ear for a straw stuck
into piercings to identify which of the children is the girl. There is a
blur of thatched roofs in the background and a fat fly perched on one of
the children's heads.

Tafara Zulu @TruthTeller1 Replying to @KayTheAuthor
~~Is the girl even real or just another of your #lies?~~
Tafara Zulu @TruthTeller1 Replying to @KayTheAuthor
Which language did you love the most?
Karen Bailey ✔ @KayTheAuthor Replying to @TruthTeller1
Bemba OFC! *Muli shani?* #EscapefromRhodesia

Ha! A greeting is as far as Google Translate will take her. Any chit-
enge-wearing tourist browsing through Pakati Sunday market can do
that. But only a native speaker can haggle with the marketers to get
what they want. So I demand the child's name instead.

Tafara Zulu @TruthTeller1 Replying to @KayTheAuthor
Ninani ishina umwana?!
Karen Bailey ✔ @KayTheAuthor Replying to @TruthTeller1
LOL! All in my memoir! Will gladly tell u bout my process,
though. I ♥ sharing that journey. #EscapefromRhodesia

> **Tafara Zulu** @TruthTeller1 Replying to @KayTheAuthor
> ~~#Liar.~~ 🙄 🙄 🙄 🙄
> **Tafara Zulu** @TruthTeller1 Replying to @KayTheAuthor
> Did YOU actually visit Zambia?
> **Karen Bailey** ✔️ @KayTheAuthor Replying to @TruthTeller1
> OFC Sweetie 😂 It's literally ALL there in the memoir.
> Reviewers are calling it pure dead brilliant, y'know! Did YOU
> actually read it, little miss reporter? #EscapefromRhodesia

JOURNALIST! I want to type. *EVELYN HONE COLLEGE GRAD-UATE.* The blue *Knowledge with Integrity* crest just above my framed diploma is the first thing you'd see walking into my mother's sitting room.

That Karen's "dead brilliant" book has no reviews on Goodreads eggs me on more than a little. No way my boss won't have this on the second page at least, unless a politician dies tonight and steals the spotlight.

> **Tafara Zulu** @TruthTeller1 Replying to @KayTheAuthor
> ~~LOL. Well, I abandoned the cheap safari tour after 50 pages of~~
> ~~"local opportunists," "primitive" and "pigeon-like" people ready~~
> ~~for "snatching and stealing." #BaileyLies~~

I'm tapping furiously now, deleting, rewording. All the while, *realignment* ricochets in my head. I snatch the words of her blurb and finally write: *What was it like, the Civil War?*

During my stint at the Zambia National Tourism Board two years ago, our number one selling point after the seventh World Wonder that is Victoria Falls was that Zambia has never had a civil war. It was the only way to convince the American tourists calling about a potential "motherland" visit that, yes, the falls were better from the Zambian side than the Zimbabwean side. And if after that assurance, they still wavered, I'd cheerfully add, "Zambia is the most peaceful country on the continent!" *One of*, but what's two missing words in the motherland? "We've never had a civil war in our fifty-year history!"

> **Karen Bailey** ✅ @KayTheAuthor Replying to @TruthTeller1
> Horrid 😞. As you can imagine! I just had 2 tell the story. The world has to know. #EscapefromRhodesia

I chuckle, but still feel this unreachable scratch at the back of my throat. It feels a little too similar to me rapidly nodding at my boss as he led me, with his hand pressed onto the small of my back, into the crammed Mulomo room.

I could have spun around easily. I could have flashed him a smile and pretended like his face, small and round, mouth overcrowded with teeth and a scraggly beard, was good to look at. I could have let him lead me to his office and do what the rumors said the other girls did to get their promotions. But I never was good at pretending.

Stay professional. What I thought to myself as the boss showed me my new desk, buried under old newspapers, dusty files, and an ancient gray computer. This time, I say the thought out loud instead of shoving it to the back of my head.

Tafara Zulu @TruthTeller1 Replying to @KayTheAuthor I can't imagine it at all. Rhodesia after all isn't a name we've used since 1964!

Tafara Zulu @TruthTeller1 Replying to @KayTheAuthor And what about the Hutu-Tutsi conflict you write about? Are you aware that it happened years before #EscapefromRhodesia? #BaileyLies

Tafara Zulu @TruthTeller1 Replying to @KayTheAuthor Are you aware that it all happened in a different country.

Tafara Zulu @TruthTeller1 Replying to @KayTheAuthor And the children you offered soft drinks? Is that the change you brought to Zambia? ~~LOL,~~ Coke?

Steve Agent @TheRealAgent Replying to @TruthTeller1 @KayTheAuthor This is Miss Bailey's agent. Please direct all further queries about her new book to the agency via our website in my bio. Thank you.

Tafara Zulu @TruthTeller1 Replying to @KayTheAuthor @TheRealAgent ~~LOL.~~ Just one thing, Steve. For the article, should we say "fiction" or "memoir?" #BaileyLies

By now, new users have joined the thread. Zambia might have never been to war, but online we can fight. My article is basically writing itself.

@ZambianPatriot has tagged five friends to witness #BaileyLies. The friends tag more friends, who ask, *Does she know English is the main language in Zambia and did she maybe mean the other Rhodesia? #AfricaIsACountry*. Someone suggests Ms. Bailey might have downed too many glasses of the liqueur of the same name. *Wrong country*, someone else chimes in. *#EuropeIsACountry*. And *LOLs* trail that.

My laptop battery is flashing red when I proofread my article a final time before going back to refresh Karen's page, to see if anything has changed.

The pinned tweet has disappeared.

You are blocked.
You can't follow or see @KayTheAuthor's Tweets. Learn More.

CHIDUNUNE

Kuwaha ca mutopa mutulo muli uleko.

A smoking pipe looks very clean on the outside, yet it is filthy on the inside.

—Luvale proverb

In an open pit of black sand, Zangi crouches next to the hill farthest from the excavators. She squints through the clouds of dust, scanning the mine. Noisy machines glisten in the sunshine as they swallow and spit chunks of earth, while miners disappear into the ditches they leave behind.

The best hiding places are in plain sight, she is thinking. That is why she ran the entire three kilometers, even though she shouldn't be there. The other children had scurried into the maize field or the rocky path to the Kaminguli River, where the rustling stalks and burbling water would mask their giggles and shuffles. But she had stolen past a snoring security guard by the crooked, rusty gate, ignored the *NO TRESPASSERS* sign, and dashed straight into Kansanshi mine.

"They won't catch me here," she whispers when a shadow suddenly looms over her. Zangi spins and finds herself face-to-face, not with her eight-year-old peer, but a gaunt man dressed head to toe in black, blending with the dirt.

"Sir," Zangi blurts, "it's just play. I'll go n-now-now." She points her forefinger downward for emphasis.

Why did I come? she thinks now, tears blurring her sight, but she stops short of crying when she recalls the taunt to the game she and her friends are playing.

Ichidunu! Chilalisha! Abaiche! Tababako! They sing it each time the game starts. *Hide-and-seek! Can make you cry! Little children! Cannot play!*

"What are you playing?" asks the man.

"*Chi-chidunune?*" Zangi stumbles over the word. "I-it's m-my time to hide? B-but, I—I'll go now." She flips her index finger to the sky to swear she is telling the truth.

She makes another attempt to apologize, all the while admonishing herself.

Why couldn't I have crawled up the baobab tree and eavesdropped on the men talking in the hembo instead? She pictures the village square, with the thick trunk in the center, its velvet-skinned fruit pulling down on its weblike branches, casting strange shadows on the faces of the men below.

Why didn't I hide among the cows in the kraal?

"Will you whip me?" Zangi whimpers, rubbing her buttocks as she braces for a lashing.

I just had to win!

"Whip you?" The man chuckles.

Hearing a statement, not a question, Zangi tries to escape, but the man seizes her wrist.

What smooth hands, Zangi thinks, contrasting the stranger's with her father's calloused fingers. Her eyes search the pit for the hard hats, hoping to spot the one on her father's head.

"Chidunune, eh?" the man repeats slowly, scratching his beard. "I used to play that one."

"Did you win?"

The man kneels to face Zangi. "I always win," he says, his narrow face unfolding a thin line of teeth.

Zangi winces, reeling from the hot stench of katata on the man's breath.

"Don't be scared. I will help you win."

Zangi wants to believe him, but her heart won't stop thumping. She turns to point toward Kampanda Village and says, "M-my house isn't f-far," even though she can't see the pointed roofs of the huts where all the food grown during the rain season is stored.

"Not before we win," answers the man, tightening his grip on Zangi's wrist.

"I'm winning, n-no one's found me."

The man brings a finger to his lips. *Shh.* "Come with me," he whispers, and lurches forward, hauling Zangi with him.

"Y-you help m-me win?"

"I'll show you a hiding place where they'll never find you."

Zangi drags her feet.

"Where w-we g-going?"

They're leaving the open pit, and beneath Zangi's bare feet, the soil is fading into the color of raw groundnuts, and the groaning and creaking of the metal against copper of Kansanshi is replaced by the rumble of tires on gravel.

"I'm supposed to be taking care of my sister!" Zangi shrieks.

"Don't you want to win?" the man demands.

Zangi nods vigorously to make up for her lie. She doesn't have a sister; all her mother's other children are dead.

"I thought so," says the man, quickening his steps.

When they stop, they are hemmed in by wild loquat trees instead of red mud huts, dry grass jutting out of the parched ground instead of thatched into roofs.

For a moment, all Zangi can feel is the throbbing in the cracks on her heels, but when she notices an ivory minibus, with the door gaping like a hippo, waiting for its dinner, the drumming in her chest starts again.

Zangi digs her toes into the ground. "Where are we?"

"I told you," says the man, killing the smile dancing in the corner of his thin lips.

"B-but M-mama will b-beat me!" She trembles.

"Quiet," says the man through gritted teeth, pulling a crumpled handkerchief from his jacket pocket and shoving it into Zangi's mouth.

He lifts Zangi, hurls her into the back of the minibus, and binds her wrists with a wire, shutting the sunlight out as he slides the door with a bang.

By the time the shock passes, Zangi can feel that the bus has navigated its way out of the stony terrain and into the pothole-riddled Chingola-Solwezi Road.

Zangi spits out the dirty cloth and starts to plead, but can't finish the sentence—her voice is runny porridge, like the smooth paste her mother stirs for her every morning.

"You make trouble, he kill you!" snaps a shrill voice stabbing the dark.

"W-who are y-you?"

"Nyaka," replies the voice. "And if we're quiet, he'll give us food and water at night."

"How will we know it's night?"

"When we stop."

"How…?" Zangi starts. "How many nights has it been for you?"

"Three?" Nyaka whispers.

Zangi nods.

When the bus finally grinds to a stop, the door slides open to let in a cocktail of sounds: hawkers rapidly talking over each other—the language bounces off her ears like a grasshopper—all the words strange; music booming; and a growling Zangi can't place.

The man carries Zangi and Nyaka onto a dusty verandah of a decrepit house, where a light flickers on, hesitating twice before flooding them in its white glow.

Zangi stares at the floor, at four bare feet, and two bigger pairs in black leather, covered in sand, stare back. Flying ants swarm around the bulb above them, drawing Zangi's eyes upward, but they land on a man whose face is as white as hyena feces. Zangi gasps and stumbles backward.

"I brought two," he says.

"A ghost!" yells Zangi.

Nyaka elbows her.

"Oow!"

"The fee," he says to the white one.

"My parents w-will look for me!" Zangi throws a fist in the air.

"Right, the fee," responds the white one, dipping his hand into his denim.

"M-m-my m-mother w-w-won't rest until sh-she finds me!"

Nyaka scoffs.

"I—I have homework today."

"Good doing business with you, boss." The man turns to leave.

"Don't l-leave—" is as many words as Zangi can mumble before the ghost shoots her a look that shuts her up. Nyaka and Zangi trail the ghostly man into the house while the bus sputters on.

Inside, he unties them and locks them in an empty room with a reed mat in the middle.

With the buzzing of the mosquitoes as a lullaby, Zangi and Nyaka squeeze onto the mat. Zangi dreams of her father kicking the door open and whipping her all the way home, but wakes to her grumbling stomach and the wind echoing through an empty house.

She rubs crust from the corner of her eyes, shoves Nyaka awake, and says "Let's run!" before her mind can cower from the idea.

"Ah, ah. You don't greet first, in your village? You just start talking without knowing if the night took anyone in their sleep?"

"Before the ghost wakes up, let's go."

Nyaka raises her head and clicks her tongue.

"Are you coming or not?"

"I want to live." Nyaka shrugs and scratches the mosquito bites on her legs until the pimples are tiny red dots.

Zangi nudges a window open, stumbling when it swings wide, but as soon as she tumbles out, her hairs stand up. This time, the looming shadow is short, panting, and growling, which soon turns into barking, spraying saliva across her back. Zangi scrambles up, races, and clambers halfway over the gate that had let the bus in and out. When she tumbles, she's face-to-face with a sharp row of teeth, growling, and spittle.

"Simba!" barks the voice behind the dog.

The accent is strange, the *a* too soft.

"Out!"

The dog, black except for two spots of brown above its eyes, slinks low but continues to growl.

Zangi's tongue, heavy in her mouth, throbs, a metallic liquid trickling down the side of her mouth like spit out of the dog's open mouth.

"Stand up!"

Zangi's not sure if she can, but slowly she rises, despite her shaking legs.

"Pull that shit again, and you die."

Nyaka watches from the window, her eyes as wide as Zangi's.

As they walk back to the house, Zangi notices a wet patch on her shorts.

Even though the window stays open, swinging in the breeze; even though the wind brings in strange and familiar sounds alike—cocks crowing good morning and fritters sizzling in hot oil; the crackle of night fires and distant police sirens; roasting groundnuts and wailing babies; boiled maize and rotting mangoes; chirping crickets and roaring radios—Zangi stays inside now, waiting to be found.

Every day, Zangi and Nyaka share a bath in a slimy green bucket until they no longer hide the spaces between their legs. They share the morsels the white one feeds them, ignoring the blandness, dried bread, fizzled-out orange drinks, cold potato slices.

Then, just when Zangi is starting to believe the man's words: *I will show you a hiding place where they will never find you*, the white man brings a woman in the house.

"Come," she says, beckoning Zangi. She's smiling, but her voice is the coldest July morning.

Zangi stays rooted to the floor, rubbing her goose pimples flat in the thick silence.

The woman places a pile of clothes and a pair of worn sneakers into her arms. "Get dressed," she says.

I must be going home, Zangi convinces herself as she gets dressed. The sleeves of her shirt could fit two more arms on each side, and the sneakers pinch her ankles as she lumbers around, but she gives the shoes a grin. Her very first pair of shoes!

"Your name is Anna," clips the woman. "You are nine years old."

"You take me home now? Y-yes? I—I show Mama my shoes."

"Your name is Anna," the woman repeats, widening her eyes at her. "You are nine years old. I am your mother."

Zangi's mouth hangs open—voice trapped.

"Do you understand me?"

She nods and gapes at the woman.

"Say it!"

She compares the woman's slim fingers, ringed on the fourth finger of her left hand, with her own mother's wide, steady palms.

"My name Anna, I—"

"Is," she interjects through gritted teeth.

"Is."

She clasps her fingers around Zangi's wrist. "Stupid. I said, your name is Anna."

The woman's skin is raw liver—no blisters across her palm like Mama.

"Your—my. M-my name *is* Anna." Her eyes, through plastic-rimmed glasses, are the pit of a well, *nothing like Mama's honeyed brown.*

Zangi repeats the rest until she smiles. The word *mother*, strange food on her tongue.

She drags Zangi out of the house and into the back of a silver car.

We must be returning home, Zangi thinks still, waving at Nyaka, who is staring out through a window, crying.

Zangi latches onto that thought as the car backs up, glides over the tar, turns onto a smooth road, and zips past glossy office blocks, and the radio flicks on. "You're listening to Phoenix FM."

"Home," she whispers to herself as they veer right, past two police checkpoints, and into a lot of cars.

"What is your name?" asks the woman, smiling at her when they arrive.

"Zangi."

She digs her long nails into Zangi's wrist.

"A-a-nna." Her voice wobbles. "I—I'm nine years old. Y-y-you a-are m-my m-mother."

"Good," she says, loosening her grip and dusting off Zangi's shoulder. She leads her into a muted white building covered in tiles.

Inside, they go through glass doors and stop in front of someone in a navy uniform. She hands the uniformed person two little books.

"Anna?" the person says.

And Zangi is surprised by how quickly she says, "Yes?"

"Are you looking forward to flying to America?"

WHERE IS JANE?

> *Wakome lyobe washa lya mubiyo lile sabala.*
> You kill yours, and leave the other person's playing about.
>
> **—Bemba proverb**

Someone is banging on the door. It shakes in protest, scattering the splinters of light that push through the cracks in the wood.

Who is it? shouts the voice in my head. But my mouth, as always, is as still as the musty air in the room I call home. I glare at the door, twice my height, and will it to stop. I fist my palms and hold my breath. Any louder, and Bupe, my brother, will wake up. But it ignores me—wretched door, and quivers again: *Nko. Nko. Nko!*

I tiptoe closer, as quiet as the colonies of roaches rummaging through our green storage bins: mealie meal, sugar, and rice—the last two of which we haven't eaten in months.

"It's me!" yells Lumbiro from the other side of the door, her shrill voice bouncing off the uneven walls. To this, the voice in my head growls, a blazing ball of sound trapped between my gut and lips. I don't want Bupe to stop snoring. If he does, he'll whimper, then explode into a ceaseless wail until Bamayo returns to shove her breast into his mouth and slap me with her free hand. My punishment for disrupting her work in Mr. Phiri's red BMW. Our one-room house, built into a fence using leftover chunks of concrete that were once building blocks for a real house, is just within her earshot.

Shh, I say to my sleeping brother with my index finger pressed on my mouth. He stirs but dreams on.

I peel the door open, as one would a scab from a sore, gently, *pano-no-panono*, yet still it groans.

"Do you want to play?" asks Lumbiro, tapping her feet, peering behind me. She knows the answer.

I can't. I shake my head. I have to take care of my brother.

She smirks, spins, and shrieks, "Nichi chibulu!" As if being mute makes me deaf too. The other children, waiting for her report a few meters away, snigger.

I'll come later, the voice in my head lies, even though I know that by the time Bamayo comes back, the other children will have retreated into their homes.

I sit on the smooth side of the block that plays veranda, leaving the door slightly ajar, and plant my chin into my palms. I lean into the shade of the corrugated roofing sheets above and watch the game unfold.

Lumbiro kneels next to another child, who will play the *mother* while the others encircle them, forming a train with their arms.

> *I want to see my Jane, my Jane, my Jane,*
> *I want to see my Jane, my Jane, Jane—Jane!* starts the song.

Jane is here! I want to yell. *Jane is me!* But when I part my lips, the words won't form.

Where is Jane?

"Jane is at school!" fibs the *mother*, hiding the *Jane*—Lumbiro behind her narrow frame.

School, I think, staring past the children. Through the gaps between the soaring blocks of weeping-white flats, over the red automobile where Bamayo is still rocking Mr. Phiri next to the fence, sits St. Patricks Girls Primary School.

I'll go one day, whispers the voice in my head, prompting my grin as I picture myself in the green checkered uniform.

> *I want to see my Jane, my Jane, my Jane,*
> *I want to see my Jane, my Jane, Jane—Jane!*
> *Where is Jane?*
> *Jane has gone to the market!* replies the *mother*.

Kabwata Market, my destination on the days Bamayo works overnight. With Bupe wrapped in a chitenge across my back, I sneak in through the rusty gate. The chain is never locked, just wrapped multiple times to give the illusion of security to the stall owners. The sounds of the night—rumba beats from the Twins Bar and wheels rumbling over the patchy tar of Ninth Street—mask the clanging metal.

When the chains detangle, my nostrils are struck by the stench: ditches brewing urine and dirty rainwater, wood singed into charcoal, burnt tufts of synthetic hair extensions. Once inside, I race past the tailoring shops, careen right into the gift shop aisle, and let the glimmering wrapping paper guide me toward the fruit-and-vegetable section. There, trusting vendors left their wares, covered in black plastic bags, sealed on four corners with rocks. My brother's eyes flicker on, and together we feast.

Carefully, I pull two cherry tomatoes from the corner of a neat pile. Out of a bucket, we choose the softest guavas. A handful of raw groundnuts and the fattest sweet potato for later, and we're ready to slink back home and creep under the blanket, where Bamayo will find us sleeping when she arrives with the rising sun the next morning.

The children continue to circle the crouching *Jane*, asking once more, "Where is Jane?"

Jane is washing the plates!

The ones waiting in a shomeka of murky water. A black fly zips over me, buzzing around the room before departing, empty-winged. I sigh and amble inside to lug the shomeka out and feed the water to the garden next to our outdoor toilet. Flaps of pumpkin leaves shading fist-sized gourds lap it up.

Under the tap that hangs from the moldy wall of our house, I scrub the plastic dishes with soil to remove the oil and food stains, then place them on a patch of grass to dry.

Where is Jane?
Jane is taking care of the baby.

My job. Taking care of my brother—the baby. Change his nappies before they scald his backside. Wipe his nose, which is always runny. Pacify him when the hunger pains make him cranky until Bamayo's reappearance.

WHERE IS JANE?

Where is Jane?
Jane is sick.

The thing I become when Bamayo brings a client home. When she parts the curtains that split the room in two and flings herself on the mattress. Bupe and I face the door and wait for the grunting to stop, but the man, fatter than the mattress, won't finish. So Bamayo, needing to feed Bupe, calls me to help. Her client grins at me, rips my skirt off, aims his snake, shoves it between my legs, and grunts until it oozes a thick liquid into me that burns when it slithers down my legs, even after he is gone.

I make Bamayo miss work the next day and many days after that because of my inability to get up in the mornings, spewing urine and blood.

I want to see my Jane, my Jane, my Jane,
I want to see my Jane, my Jane, Jane—Jane!

Their faces are now twisted in sadness over *Jane's* affliction.

Where is Jane?
Jane is in the hospital.

A filthy word describing the place to which we arrive, Bamayo, Bupe, and me.

The word *hospital* drips in my head like blood from a wound refusing to heal.

Hospital is the disgusting look on the nurse's face when she touches me through her latex gloves.

It is the doctor quizzing my mother—what's wrong—while keeping his eyes fixed on his clipboard.

You know children. My mother shrugs.

Hmph, replies the doctor, his eyes glued to the sheet.

She just started urinating on the bed, says Bamayo.

Defilement, mutters the nurse, scrunching her nose. Together with *hospital,* the letters of *defilement* crawl on my skin, like the maggots on our toilet floor, making me scratch.

No. Bamayo shakes her head vigorously, not minding that her curly wig might fall and show the scruffy lines of mukule under which she hides her hair. *I'm not married,* she explains. *It's just my children and me. This one has been a sickler from birth,* a truth she makes me confirm by bulging her eyes.

Sickler, screams the voice in my head.

Yes. I nod.

The doctor lifts his gaze to stare at me. *Jane, did someone hurt you?*

Yes! screeches the voice in my head. *No.* I shake it.

The doctor weighs this, scribbles something, and proceeds to the next sick child.

> *I want to see my Jane, my Jane, my Jane,*
> *I want to see my Jane, my Jane, Jane—Jane!*

A mournful song this time—hunched backs and downcast eyes, mimicking women approaching the telltale army-green tent pitched outside a funeral house.

The climax of the game is fast approaching, and the children, braced for it, edge farther from the center, where the *Jane* is now lying in the dirt, eyes closed and head limp on her arms as pillows. The *mother* is wringing her fingers, begging the skies for a miracle.

Now Bamayo hovers over me. "Jane," she pleads, tears streaking her flawless skin. "Buka!" she screams—wake up!

I'm trying to hold her begging eyes but find myself drawn instead into the blinding light of the ceiling. The scents of the ward are pungent all of a sudden. The windows swing, bringing in the sweet breeze of nature, trying to overpower the stench of what looms. Now the sounds roar; singing crickets howl, scratching my eardrums raw. Bupe's snore is a strange thunder on a March night such as this.

I tremble.

Finally, when my lids tire, press shut, comes peace in a familiar tune, now a slow, low drone.

Where is Jane?

The question halts the noise, diffuses the smells, and in the blackness, I smile.

Jane is dead.

ACKNOWLEDGMENTS

I am so fortunate to have this many people to thank for the stories in this collection. I could not have done it without you. Thank you to the following people and organizations:

My love, Rachael Hope Banda, I am okay and I hope you are proud.

My Bijou, Theresa Sylvester, for every phone call, every re-read, every tear-filled silence, every laugh, every deconstruction of the brutal things we endured as children, everything, thank you, dear wanga. So, ndiye so.

Rungano Nyoni, the sister who chooses me every day; for 1999, for the Show that day, for shoes, for coming to the rescue, for being my advocate even when I didn't deserve it, and for Y. I am a writer because you were so, so sure. Natotela wemukalamba wandi.

My grandma, Renée Nanchengwa-Nglazi. Kaapa, ndalumba, for holding me while I healed, for giving me the space to fly, to create. This book exists because you exist.

Foday Mannah, whose steady and relentless encouragement kept me going on the hard days. Thank you for insisting that the fourth time would be the charm—you were right.

Afua Quarshie of the Hubert H. Humphrey (Fulbright) Fellowship, for supporting me throughout my fellowship and ever since, and especially for seeing "Where Is Jane?" Thanks also to one of my host parents that year, Caroline Schultz, for asking the necessary questions, and the 2018/2019 fellows who read some of these stories and helped me develop them—Inbar Ben Menda, Lucy Rumbidzai Chivasa, Mariana Machado, and Zintle Koza.

My creative writing mentors, Ellen Banda-Aaku and Sheila O'Connor, for mentioning my name in important places, giving advice when needed, and always being on call.

My first editor, Kathy Bosman, who saw many of these stories in their worst selves, for always making time.

Stan Jacobson and everyone at the Hawkinson Peace Fund Scholarship for believing in this collection, what it says, and what it stands for, and for generously funding the dream.

Everyone at the Africa Institute in Sharjah, where most of these were cleaned up, for gifting me the space and time to write.

My brilliant, beautiful friends in the HMR (ishina ni nkama yesu aini girls?) WhatsApp group—Anastasia Shandele, Chipo Dandawa, Claudia Lozintha Hamukale, Irene Mtaja-Chiyesu, Joan Mtaja, Louise Amoni, Hon. Mwiinga Simaanya, Mwila Kasonde-Anamela, Ngambo Mukanda, and Precious Musonda—for sharing all those wonderful stories that helped breathe life to mine.

The Kitana Book Club, for inspiration, spirited discussions, and moral support, and especially Lenganji Mainza Haakantu for never letting me or my stories go.

ACKNOWLEDGMENTS

All the teachers at the Voodoonauts Summer Workshop who helped me step out of my genre comfort zones and create something new.

My professors at Hamline University's Creative Writing Programs, especially Brian Malloy, John Brandon, Mike Alberti, and Richard Pelster-Wiebe. Thanks also to all my MFA classmates, especially Lydia Hansen, Kristin Boldon, Megan Chua, Mikayla Johnson, and Vickie McCurdy, for all the thoughtful feedback.

My literary friends who have read, listened, encouraged, shared opportunities, and let me sulk when necessary—A. K. Herman, Dr. Chido Muchemwa, Emma Shercliff, Frances Ogamba, Fiske Serah Nyirongo, Greta Huttanus, Kasimma, Keletso Mopai, Mbozi Haimbe, Peter Ngila, Rémy Ngamije, Rešoketšwe Manenzhe, Ukamaka Olisakwe, Zanta Nkumane, and Zenas Ubere.

My patient readers—Brittany Kerschner, Chilufya Musekwa Mumba, Chinga Kalwani Zimba, Dorica Banda, Dr. Kapula Chifunda, Kamana Sharon Kamwengo Katawola, Kudakwashe Khuleya, Lynette Walubita, Dr. Patience Phiri-Nseluka, and Violet Nanchengwa.

My word wardens, who translate when memory fails or I venture beyond my mother tongues: Thank you, Eunice Banda Mwale, Fydes Banda-Mvunga, Hellen Banda-Mutale, Justice Susan Mtonga-Wanjelani, Scariot Elisha Banda, Phillip Elisha Banda, Reverend Elisha Banda III, Florence M. Mbewe, Linah Daizy Zulu, Mukuma Chilila Chipawa, and Waicha Ndhlovu-Yambala, for every translation.

My young Kaapa, Mulenga Kaite Simaanya, for all the makani.

Dr. Alma Nalisha Cele of the *Cheeky Natives*, at first interviewer, at last friend, who insisted on this collection.

Angie Cruz, for believing in and selecting the manuscript.

The phenomenal team of the University of Pittsburgh Press—Jane

McCaffery, Peter Kracht, Melissa Dias-Mandoly, John Fagan, Eileen Louise O'Malley, Amy Sherman, Kelly Lynn Thomas, Lesley Rains, Alex Wolfe, and Caleb Gill—for giving my book such a loving home, and Christine Ma, for her copyediting.

I am sure I have forgotten someone, but not because I am not grateful. Thank you to everyone who helped these stories become exactly what they needed to be.

Stories previously appeared in journals, sometimes in earlier forms: "Azubah" and "A Doctor, a Lawyer, an Engineer, or a Shame to the Family" in *adda*; "Inswa" in the *Kalemba Short Story Prize* and *Exhale: African Queer Anthology*, "Reflections" in *Aiden Shaw's Penis & Other Stories of Censorship*; "Do Not Hate Me." in *Make Your Presence Known*: *Stories of Seances, Conjuring, and Mediumship*; "Hail Mary" in *Dreamers Creative Writing*; "Mastitis" in the *Doek Anthology*; "Speaking English,*" translated into Italian in *Menelique Magazine*; "It Will Be Beautiful Again" in *Doek! Literary Magazine*; "Chidunune" in *Two Sisters Writing and Publishing*; and "Where is Jane?" in the *Airgonaut*.